Printed by CreateSpace, An Amazon.com Company.
Available from Amazon.com and other retail outlets.

ISBN 10: 1535124490
ISBN 13: 978-1535124492

Does This Knife Make Me Look Fat?

by

William A Sloan

This first attempt at a novel
is dedicated to
Mary,
who was there on the first day
and encouraged me to go for it,

and to
Murphy,
who was there throughout
the process
and encouraged me to continue.

Prologue

A little splash of color.

"Perfect," she said, "and done."

Carla Montgomery was ready to go. Anything that didn't land in her Balenciaga knapsack, she could buy when she got there. Bucks County on a Friday for a fundraiser. Seriously? What a girl does for some people.

She grabbed her clutch, phone, iPad, charger and keys, turned out the lights and opened the door.

"Hello Carla."

She was surprised to see her visitor, but happily so.

"Hello you! This is unexpected. Running late as usual. My car's waiting downstairs," she said, as she offered her cheek for a kiss. She never saw the knife.

Carla fell into a pile of high-end leather goods, technology and Tom Ford. She died quickly, quietly.

"So abstract," said the killer, "Perfect. And done."

1. So, Here We Are

It begins.

It's a Friday night around 5:00 and Kate – my best friend, sidekick, Ethel to my Lucy or is it the other way around – has just pulled into the driveway. She left the city at 2:00 after a day, no, a week of stupidity wrapped in arrogance cloaked in irrelevance – i.e., marketing. Apparently, she hit traffic or a tree, because three hours is an hour too long. From the rapidly escalating terseness of her texts, I'd say she's, um, a little tense.

I'm Able Ryder. I paint. Realist/Impressionist with an Abstract Expressionist brush stroke. I have a Minimalist sensibility with a touch of the Baroque. Did I leave anything out? One of the ironies of being an artist is that everyone wants you to be totally unique yet easily categorize-able at the same time. Funny, that. Suffice it to say, I'm very visual and aesthetically diverse.

I like people, which is helpful if you do portrait work, which, sometimes, I do. And they seem to feel comfortable with me, to the point that they tell me all kinds of personal things. Things that are certainly none of my business. Often they say, "Can you keep a secret?" and I tell them simply, "No." But they go on anyway. Business affairs, financial affairs, affairs of the heart, affairs involving other anatomical parts...they go on.

So be it.......................

I greet Kate at the door, martini in hand. She drops her bags and grabs the glass.

"Nice to see you too," I say.

She looks over the rim of the glass and between swallows says, "I'll get to you in a minute. Priorities you know..." Very Myrna Loy. She closes her eyes, sighs heavily, then re-opens and looks at me as if for the first time. "Able!" she exclaims followed by a big hug,"It's been hell! Don't even ask, I don't want to talk about it, it's sooo good to be here in Hooterville, away from all the, NO! I said I didn't want to talk about it. But you won't believe how awful it's been, I mean really awful! The stupid people are winning! It's just not right. You look great, by the way. What's for dinner?"

She has arrived.

2. And Breathe

Clink!

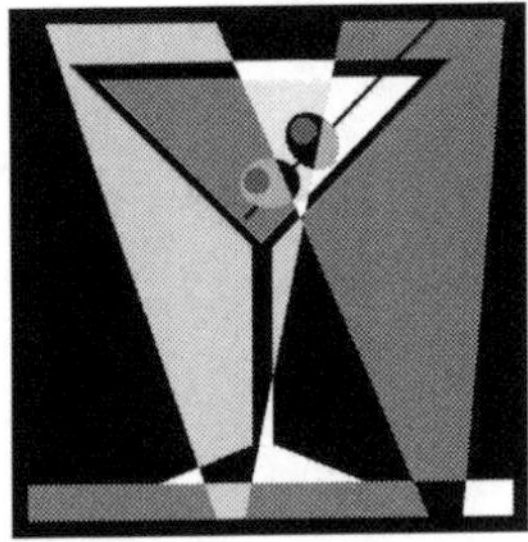

Kate, Kate Lindsey, lives and works in Manhattan, but spends many of her weekends in the country with me. We've known each other since time began and still love each other in spite of too many things to mention. We've shared big successes; dismal failures; health, wealth and stealth scenarios. We are each other's champion, confidant and safe place. Everyone should have a Kate. But there's only one. And she's mine.

"Ah, nectar from the gods. I'll be ready for a refill momentarily. Don't go anywhere."

"Just going to get my glass. You know I hate seeing anyone drink alone."

"That's just one of the many things I love about you, Able." She follows me into the great room, kicks off her Manolos and gets cozy on a bar stool. "And this is one of the others," she says, reaching across the counter to the tray of hors d'oeuvres. "Why is it," she says between chews and swallows, "when you put out nibble food it looks like a Renaissance still life; and when I put out nibble food it looks like leftovers from a soup kitchen?"

"It's a gift. What can I say? You have other talents." I join her on a bar stool, cocktail at the ready.

"Not this week I don't. Not a one. No, wait, I take that back. Is putting up with idiot clients a talent?"

"Quite a big one, and it pays well, I might add."

"This is true," again she sighs,"but I hate them anyway. I hate them all. I think they should die."

"Is this about the cosmetics account, or the car account, or the fashion account?"

"What difference does it make? They're all the same. The whole world is run by MBAs with a lot of attitude and no imagination, who wouldn't know an idea if it came gift-wrapped with a flashing neon sign attached that said 'IDEA INSIDE'.

"I spent the better part of this week in brainstorming meetings, and I use the phrase as a euphemism. Twenty very young, very expensively dressed, very overpaid vice-presidents of something-or-other sat around the way-over-designed conference table in what once was our conference room, but is now called *Concept Central*, I kid you not, complete with a sign and everything; while a forty-something captain of the cheerleaders type, if the cheerleaders happen to be completely without cheer and totally lacking in leadership abilities, stood at an easel-mounted sketch pad, which is an insult to you and every artist since Giotto, and with an obscenely large marker in her hot little fist, reciting the old adage, a favorite of mine and, I know, one of yours – *There is no such thing as a bad idea* – over and over and over again until Monday became Tuesday and Tuesday became Wednesday and so on and so on, which brings us to the end of a week, with not one word uttered by 16 of the 20 people in the room, not one idea deemed 'quite right' by Our Lady of the Marker, with several expensive client lunches consumed, and an ad campaign launch date that's gaining on me even as I speak!"

Kate finally comes up for air and a large swallow of her martini, emptying the glass in the process. She exaggeratedly peers into the glass with one eye shut, then lifts it by the stem and shakes it in my direction, looking at me like a forlorn waif.

"Would the lady like another?"

"Oh, I couldn't possibly," she says, sliding the empty glass over in front of me.

As I move to replenish her drink, I ask, "Do you feel better now?"

"A bit." She fixes herself a little paté on a cracker. "It's never any different. I know that. It's just, sometimes it gets to me more than others. Oh, I'm too old for this nonsense."

"Not too old. Never too old. You're bored. And you're on the verge of burning out. What you need is to be spoiled for a few days. I can manage that. And you need something completely different to challenge your remaining brain cells. I think I can arrange that, too."

"Able, Able, Able. What would I do without you?"

"You'd probably be living on Tic-Tacs and contemplating life as a serial killer." I hand Kate her second martini.

"I'll drink to that."

"I had a feeling you would." We clink glasses and begin to settle into the weekend. "We still have plenty of time, so just relax."

Clearly, my last comment has her confused.

"We're going out later. Remember?"

"Of course...Opening?"

"Costume party/Fundraiser."

"Right...The Michener Museum?"

"The Audubon Society."

"Right....do we have to dress like birds or something? Feathers would be considered bad taste at an Audubon event, I suppose..."

"One would think. Birds are the theme, though."

"Well, that's just wrong, and I'm certainly not one to tempt fate," she pauses just long enough to swallow yet another super-sized something-on-a-Ritz," *So* good! Couldn't we just stay here and keep eating everything on this platter? This is a-maz-ing!"

"No. Glad you like the spread, though. Every chef needs an appreciative audience."

"There! That's my talent this week. I'm a terrific appreciative audience."

"The best in the business."

"Oh, Able. It's so good to be here. You always know just what to say and do. Marry me?"

"Sure thing. How about next Thursday?"

"Okay...Oh, wait. Thursday's not good for me. The cable guy's coming."

"Some other time then."

We look at each other lovingly; two friends secure in our shared affection.

"So, what are we wearing to this bird thing? I have an idea..."

"Of course you do. Drink up and let it marinate."

I'd been a full-time New Yorker for years – black leather furniture, black wardrobe, black coffee, black moods – sometimes, it was easier to let the veneer do the talking when you, yourself, had nothing to say. My work was successful but stale – big, black, overly-intellectualized squares. Constructivist. Minimal. In truth, empty.

Ten years ago it all changed. I was out to dinner with friends at some new restaurant of the moment. The room was ugly, the waiter rude, the music numbing and the very expensive food, in its meager little ant-sized portions, awful. When I overheard a neighboring diner say that the silver cube salt and pepper shakers were, "...too divine, so neo-Bauhaus, very important!" with no sense of irony, I realized I'd had enough.

I escaped to Bucks County, Pennsylvania, where I found a rambling old farmhouse that I crammed full with rugs and pots and pictures and things, all kinds of things. Lots of color, lots of activity, more than a little humor. Kind of the anti-New York residence. It was home.

The only thing I held onto from back then and there, was my friendship with Kate. She got the whole early mid-life crisis thing and never judged, or if she did, she didn't tell me. She was always there to champion the cause, mix cocktails, listen to my endless rantings and ravings...or even just share the quiet. Thanks in no small part to her, I "came back to the light," as she put it. And she got a weekend place in the country.

I began to work again. My paintings took on a whole new look – they were good. My New York gallery dropped me, naturally. But I found another – The Hugo Swann Gallery in Chelsea – and my first show there was a success. This time I felt like I'd earned it.

Kate said, "Maybe there really is something to that whole artists-have-to-suffer thing."

I said, "Maybe, or maybe they just have to be honest."

"Maybe," she replied, "or maybe they just have to be good."

"Thank you."

"You're welcome."

3. What's News?

Everyone's a critic.

Kate continues to nurse her cocktail and lower her blood pressure while stabbing at cheeses and patés...ok, maybe I was wrong about lowering the blood pressure...and perusing the *Times* – some of today's, some from this past week, all piled high on the bar stool next to hers. I love the *Times*, the print version...old school...but that sound of the rustling papers is so key...

"Able, listen to this." Kate folds back the front page of last Sunday's *Arts and Leisure* section and clears her throat with a practiced sense of drama. *"To this critic's eye, the best painting in the show is* Opus 47, *a dark, brooding work that combines Diebenkorn's structural clarity with deKooning's psychological density..."*

"A Carla Montgomery review," I interrupt,"the evening is complete. And don't get my paper wet! You know I hate that."

She sticks her tongue out, moves her cocktail, and glares at me over her Corinne McCormack cat's-eye readers, *"...it has the anger of Kline, the vitality of early Pollock, the majesty of Nevelson..."*

"I think she likes it."

"...the spiritual reverberations of Rothko and the monumental restraint of..."

"Let me guess, Motherwell?"

"Yes! Motherwell. How did you know?"

"Monumental restraint is always Motherwell."

"If you say so...*look no further. This* <u>*is*</u> -- and the <u>is</u> is underlined -- *abstract art!*...and she ends with an exclamation point."

"Really? Well, there's one thing I'll say about a Carla Montgomery review. She certainly makes you feel something."

"And you feel..."

"Thirsty! And ready for a refill. You?"

"Only if it has the vitality of early Pollock and the majesty of Nevelson."

"That can be arranged."

I tip the pitcher, fill the glasses and skewer a few olives. Kate shields her glass from the decorative vegetation.

"Let's not make it a salad, shall we? Now...who can we toast?"

"Douglas Reinhardt, I should think."

"And he would be..."

"The psychologically structural artist we just read about."

"Brilliant! To Douglas Reinhardt. He is abstract art, exclamation point!"

"So," I say, pointing my olive at Kate's glass, "is it everything you ever dreamed?"

"Vital and majestic, sir. It has the clarity of Windex and the neatness of Betty Furness."

"In addition to the Pollock/Nevelson thing?"

"Goes without saying. And now I must remove myself to prepare for the night's festivities. Able, do you think our Ms. Montgomery will be there?"

"Good chance. Nan Gibson's in charge of this shindig and they're friends, so..."

"Very fancy! Well I hope she shows. Much as I hate the witch, we could ask her all about *abstract art exclamation point!*"

"What are you wearing?" I ask.

"Whatever's in this bag. Birds are the theme you said? Then a bird it shall be."

4. Birds of a Feather

Taking flight.

Coming down the stairs, Kate is a vision in white, form-fitting Badgley Mishka. She's reaching into her LV clutch, when I say to her, "You happened to have that in your bag?"

"I like to be prepared."

"Stunning sweetie, but what are you supposed to be?"

She pulls out a small, ruby brooch in the shape of a cross – a red cross. She hands it to me and says, "Florence Nightingale. Obviously. Help me pin this on, would you?"

She turns around and reveals the lack of a back of the dress, "Centered...low."

"Bringing comfort to the afflicted?"

"We live in hopes."

Kate turns back around and studies me from head to toe. White tie and tails with a small silver silhouette of a bird on the lapel. "Care to explain?" she asks.

"Maitre D at the Stork Club. Obviously."

She smiles appreciatively. "We totally nailed this. And no feathers."

5. Feed the Birds

What's the pecking order?

By the time we arrive, the party is in full dissimulation, which is a fancy way of saying it looks like a flock of birds. Here a stork, there a flamingo, and seemingly everywhere, women claiming to be swans. Did you know swans waddle when they're on dry land?

Dissimulation, according to Webster's, also means, "a form of deception, in which one conceals the truth." Interesting, as it turns out.

The event is being held at one of Bucks County's most impressive estates – stone manor house, six or seven outbuildings, a bank barn the size of Rhode Island and acres and acres of picture perfect, rolling farm lands.

"What do they grow here?" asks Kate.

"Curiosity and envy," I answer. "But they're very nice people, really."

"You actually know them on a personal level?"

"Nan and Walter Gibson. She's old Philadelphia money and he's..."

"I *know* who the Gibsons are. Former head of UTel, socialite wife, both richer than god, huge philanthropists. Legends in their own time. And I repeat...you actually know them on a personal level?"

"Her more than him. Walter's not around much. Always off making a deal somewhere. He's not very social and doesn't like this kind of circus at all. He'd rather write a check and be done with it. Nan, on the other hand, loves it. She's the ring master, or mistress, as the case may be.

She likes to set the stage and cast the party – a little New York, a little Palm Beach, a little Hollywood, lots of locals – to her, society is theater; a valuable and vital form of entertainment and commerce requiring an attractive, energetic ensemble who know their lines and know when to enter and leave the stage. Since she's running the show, she's always looking for talented new players to fit in somewhere, breathe life into the proceedings and replace those who are on their way out. I'm kind of like her pet "Creative" out here – the presentable itinerant artist.

At which point, Nan comes over to bestow her blessing. She's wearing vintage Saint Laurent and is kind-of-spectacular. "Mr. Ryder...and Ms. Lindsey, if I'm not mistaken? Welcome! And thank you for respecting the bird population we're actually trying to save." Then she smiles a big, beautiful, what's-wrong-with-these-people smile. "Able, there's something I'd like to speak with you about. Could you and Ms. Lindsey come by tomorrow? Shall we say 1?" I nod in agreement. "And now I must circulate and try to make sure no one molts into the caviar..." As she's gliding away, Nan touches Kate's arm, "Florence Nightingale...Fabulous!"

"She's something! How does she know who I am or who I'm pretending to be?"

"Nan knows everything. She's always ten steps ahead. Speaking of which..."

Kate and I wander through the crowd, waving to this one, nodding to that one, hugging the attractive ones, always in search of the bar, like everybody else. We get many compliments and confused looks whenever we explain our costumes, which stand out in a room filled with plumage and spandex. Most people took the theme literally, apparently not realizing that, what may look good on a 19-year-old-sculpted-within-an-inch-of-his-or-her-life-Cirque-du-Soleil-contortionist, is not necessarily flattering on your-average-every-day-upwardly-mobile-socially-reaching-pharmaceutical-executive-or-his-or-her-spouse.

"Is it too early to call 'Fowl'?" smirked Kate, "When I said that I was doing Florence Nightingale to that sitting duck over there, she said, *She's one of my favorite designers.* Bless her beaky little head..." Kate's eyes keep moving to the most attractive men in the room – the cater-waiters, "Who's a girl have to pluck around here to get a martini?"

"Don't ruffle your feathers, Flo, libation is almost within reach. And don't fraternize with the kindergarten set. That could be dangerous."

"For me or for them?"

6. Face Time

Not everyone has a "good side."

"So, how many of these bird-people are your former or current portrait subjects?" Kate wants to know.

"Well, I painted Nan's two daughters...and her favorite horse."

"There's a joke in there somewhere..."

"Pace yourself. The night is young and bursting with possibilities. Let's see, there's the Scanlon family over by the dance floor – horse people – dressed as chickens I think; Marcia Bingham – lawyer, marathoner, really sweet, needs to eat a meal now and then – a flamingo maybe?; Dr. Sherman and Dr. Finch who are with their wives – a gaggle of geese, funny – talking to Nan right now, lovely people; the Bird-in-the-Gilded-Cage over there – Becka Conrad, by way of New York. Social charity girl."

"She's pretty."

"She's a bitch."

"Then she's a pretty bitch."

"She'd agree with you. Her husband, Victor, is a big deal hedge fund guy. He's over by the ice sculpture of a melting penguin, dressed as a........something blue and tight."

"Handsome."

"Nice guy too. Smart, Funny."

"Handsome, smart and funny with a chest you could bounce coins off of..."

"What?"

"Oh, nothing."

"Let's see, who else...the tight black-sequined guy over there. I'm gonna guess he's supposed to be a raven...or Liza Minnelli. He's Sean Patrick, the design star of the moment."

"Never met him but I've seen his picture everywhere. He's better looking in person, if that's possible. The eyelashes alone...he just blinked and I felt a breeze."

"He's a great guy. I've painted him, too, and he's hooked me up with a few of his clients, including Becka Conrad. He was doing their country place in Solebury. I wonder where Carla is? Shawn and Carla are usually inseparable at these things."

"Well, I'm sure she's here somewhere. She wouldn't miss the opening of a car door if it meant getting her picture on *Radar*. Did you look under the auction table?"

"And how do you really feel about her, Ms. Nightingale?"

"Way beyond beautiful, but Philadelphia Main Line or not, that bitch'll cut ya."

"That's my girl. Jane Austen had nothing on you."

7. What am I Bid?

Is it really worth all that?

Is anyone really comfortable at a party? I wonder. Is anyone really themselves at a party? Absolutely not. We're all doing a good deed by being here, which lets everyone off the hook, I guess. People use lots of innuendo...when they shouldn't, dance suggestively... when they shouldn't, flirt inappropriately...when they shouldn't. And tonight many are dressed as birds.

"Can we go now?" whines Kate.

"Not having fun, Flo?"

"You know how I feel about these kinds of things. The highlight of my evening was getting dressed. And waiter Number 4" – she waves in the direction of a handsome young man, accent on the young, carrying a tray of canapés. "Definitely a highlight. But I'm done. You?"

"Likewise." Another handsome, young man with a tray is suddenly next to us and giving me a one-arm hug.

"Great to see you Able. Drinks Thursday, okay?" and then he's gone.

"Waiter Number 5? Your highlight?"

"Possibly."

8. Last Tango in Plumsteadville

And.....dip.

"Where are we going? It's early yet and I'm not even one sheet to the wind, let alone three."

We're driving north, into the night. All dressed up and no place to go.

"Things shut down early out here. It's the country, remember?" I turn on the radio to a Latin music station. "Let's go home. I'll make omelettes and Manhattans! We can play accordion music and tango, or watch old episodes of *That Girl*..."

"Tango, please. But you have to promise to dip."

"Was there ever a question?"

We dance sometimes. Not well, but who cares? It's fun. It's fancy. It's make believe. Especially the tango. We even took classes and you know what? That stuff is hard. But very good exercise and you can't beat the music.

When we tango, my name is Javier and Kate's is Violeta. I run a tobacco shop and she paints figurines. We take our fantasy lives very seriously...for about ten minutes or so and then we dip...and then we laugh. Very fancy.

9. Lost Connection

Hello...

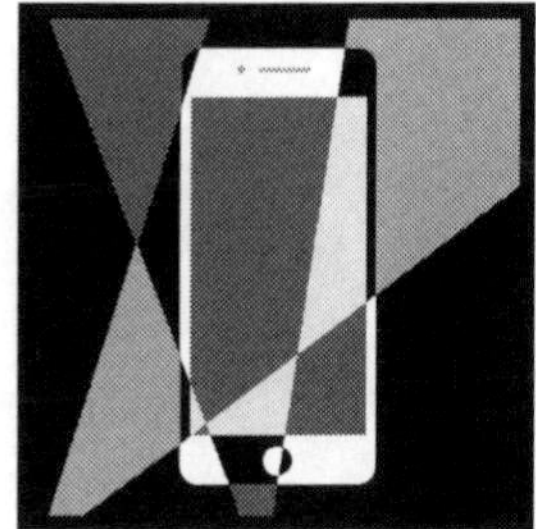

As we're driving, my phone rings. Actually it does a little mambo thing. I pick it up and see Nan Gibson's face looking at me.

"Nan! Wonderful evening!" Kate gives me an evil eye.

"Thank you, Able. But..............something's happened," long pause.

"Nan? What is it?"

"...........Carla's dead."

"What?!"

"I just heard from Sean. She was found at her apartment. She'd been stabbed." Nan sounds composed but only on the surface.

"My god! That's awful!"

Kate whispers in the background,"What? What?" I hold up my hand as Nan continues.

"She was expected at Sean's late this afternoon and then the party. Carla's always late... was...so, when she hadn't arrived, he went on without her, expecting her to meet him there. Sean's devastated, of course. It's terrible, just terrible. He asked me to get in touch with a few people. I must go.............Carla...gone...she finally met her match. Good night Able."

10. Midnight Snack

Maybe we'll just use forks.

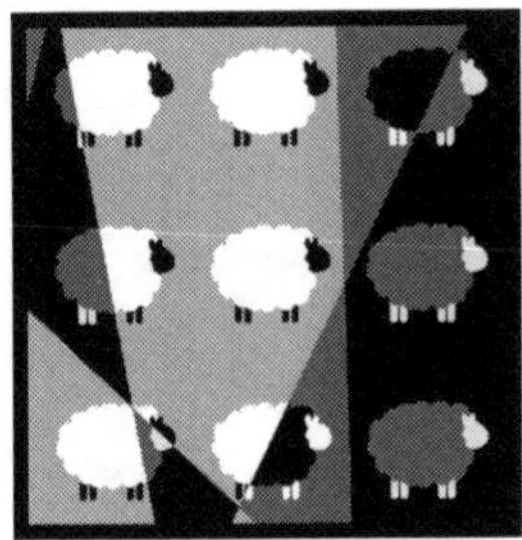

Kate has gone off to change into something more...something less...we'll have to wait and see.

I'm in my sweats, making omelettes – a little smoked gouda, a few chopped tomatoes, some mushrooms, lots of herbs; and Manhattans. Sounds like a plan.

"Smells like salvation!" she's back, in sheep covered flannels with feet and a trap door. "I hope you used the big glasses, we have lots to talk about! When you offer up *something different*, you do not disappoint! Murder and Manhattans! I love it here!

"So. Carla Montgomery. Tell me. Tell me everything. What do you know? What do you think? Were you still in touch at all? I know that was a long time ago, but you've always had a "door's always open" policy, even for the most despicable vermin. That would be her."

Apparently my eyebrow shoots up a few inches.

"What?" she continues,"You can forgive and forget if you want, but she used everyone she ever knew, *including* you. Cold-hearted, opportunistic narcissist, she got what she deserved. Start at the beginning. Let's rebuild the story and don't leave anything out... is that smoked gouda?"

11. About Carla

Nearly perfect.

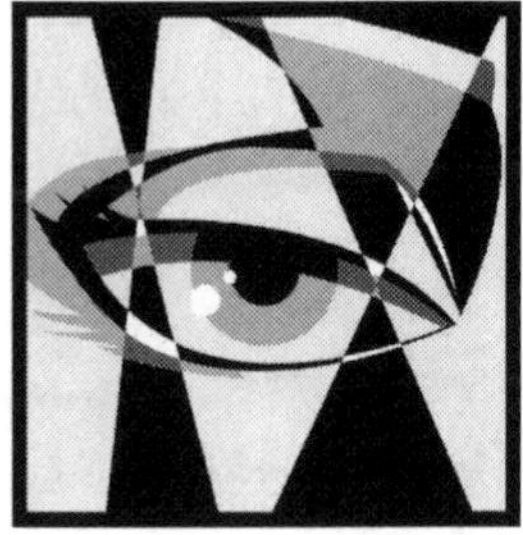

Historically, there is always someone – a beauty with brains, a body with a voice – someone who changes the atmosphere when she arrives...and sucks the air out of the room when she leaves. Different, daring, fun to watch, never to be crossed. Carla Montgomery is that woman for now...or was. She lived by her own rules. No excuses made. No explanations offered.

She came from money – the Chase Montgomerys of Philadelphia. She'd dropped the Chase from her name while in college...she had her reasons. Her mother is imposing, her father, irrelevant except for his name. Apparently, she took after mom. Educated at Vassar, then Yale, then Oxford, always with honors, always with notoriety – there was inevitably a professor, you see, and usually a married one at that.

There was a moment several years ago in New York, that's where I first met her, when she was suddenly everywhere. Some people climb the ladder to success. She took the elevator, non-stop. Somehow, through various connections, she landed a job with the Times *and as quickly as you can say, "Your wife doesn't have to know," she was the lead art critic and protector of all things cultural.*

Unlike most other art critics, she arrived at openings wearing couture. Unlike most cultural attachés, she would leave museum galas early to party at dive bars on the lower east-side. Her taste in men was as varied as everything else about her resumé – this week a silver haired diplomat from Venezuela, next week a tatted-up biker boy from the Bowery. She was photographed everywhere, her fashion sense was noted and envied, her scope of knowledge was impressive, and she liked a nasty good time. Carla was it.

For fun or out of boredom or just because she could, Carla liked using her power and considerable charms to discover talents, build careers, start trends. And as long as her interest was held, she was the best ally imaginable. However, when she tired of the game, and she always did, the new find was forgotten about...and replaced.

I played the part of pawn-to-queen-four several years ago now. We met at a friend's opening. She was already somewhat familiar with my work, or said she was. I was very familiar with everything about her. I was also, shall we say, conflicted, but she was more than a little something. I made her laugh – always good. We knew some of the same people – always helpful. We were both there alone – always convenient. It was getting late – done deal.

We had a good time for a month or so. In addition to some very creative nighttime aerobics, she decided she could further my career, get me connected, write me up, all that stuff. And she did...for a month or so. Then she met Juan Carlos and suddenly developed a taste for salsa and tequila. My internship was over. Just like that. I didn't mind really. It wasn't as if it was a surprise or anything. But it was literally over night that I became not of her world.

Juan Carlos lasted a week. After him came, oh I don't know, pick a name, she probably had one. None of them mattered. Relationships didn't matter. Not to Carla. She was cold and she was clear. No drama, no heartache. Next?

12. Missed Manners

Never underestimate the power of a well-placed *Please* or *Thank you.*

Kate is curled up on a bar stool, running her finger around the rim of her glass. "You know, I met her seven or eight times. And each time was like the first...for her. She never remembered me and let's face it, I'm not *that* easy to forget. Disappointing really, because a powerful-smart-beautiful woman, a credit to her species – you want her to be everything."

"Maybe too much to ask? Maybe everybody wanted her to be everything..."

"Not as much as *she* wanted to be everything. She didn't have to hug me like we were long-lost sorority sisters but a few steps short of rudeness would've been nice. That's all."

"True. A year after we'd had our mini-fling, I saw her at a MoMA thing and went over to say hi. She was very cordial, then asked where we knew each other from."

"Ouch."

"Actually, it seemed funny in a completely humbling and wrong sort of way. I said, *'We had great sex last year, for about a month.'*"

"What did she say?"

"Thank you."

13. Friends Indeed

Who knew?

It's the next day, and we're on our way over to Nan Gibson's for, I'm not sure what. Nan said 1:00, so 1:00 it is. She didn't say brunch, so brunch it's not.

When we arrive, Nan greets us at the door wearing khakis and a white T-shirt, looking the way every woman wants to look in khakis and a white T-shirt. No make-up, no shoes, no jewelry except a simple wedding band. Perfect. No big nouveau-flash for this lady.

She takes our hands warmly and leads the way through her home to a very big, very bright sun room.

"Feel free to put your sunglasses back on, Ms. Lindsey. I won't be offended. I love the light. It reveals everything," then she smiles. "I know Able's used to it but it can be tough for a newcomer."

Kate had been reaching for her sunglasses but puts them back in her bag. "If he can take it, so can I. I just wish I'd made up for this light."

Nan laughs. "You're very pretty, Ms. Lindsey, whatever the lighting."

"Thank you, Mrs. Gibson. And you look amazing! And no work done, am I right?"

"Kate!" I say in an all too familiar exasperated tone.

"What? I mean, I'm right, aren't I? That's all you?"

Fortunately, Nan laughs again, bigger this time. "Yes, this is the real me. I'm too low-maintenance for procedures. What you see is what you get, much like yourself, I'm guessing. And may I call you Kate? Now that we've compressed two lunch dates and a museum outing into a few seconds, I feel like we already know each other well."

"Yes please! And may I call you Nan? I'd love that!"

"Of course. You're a breath of fresh air, Kate."

"Did you hear that Able? I'm a breath of fresh air."

"One person's air is another person's wind."

"It's obvious you two adore each other," says Nan,"Wonderful to see. You don't get a lot of real, genuine friendships these days. Everyone seems to be looking for an *in* or a connection or something I don't quite understand...which leads us, I suppose, to Carla.

"Originally, Able, when I asked you to come by today, I'd wanted to talk to you about her, but in a different light – or maybe it's not a different light at all. You see, I wanted your thoughts on whether or not I should include Carla in something I'm considering and I knew you'd be honest with me." She turns to Kate and continues, "Putting personalities together is always a bit of a chess match and one of the things I love about your friend is that he knows everybody and tries hard not to judge any of them. As a result everyone tells him everything, so he knows who truly gets along with whom."

"And it's always been true," Kate interjects,"hasn't it Able? Just so you know, Nan, because I'm sure you've wondered, he's not as nice as you think. I used to worry that people took advantage of him and that he was kind of a pushover...but not so much, as it turns out. He's got this steel door thing that happens..."

"Hello," I say, "Still in the room," I say.

"Go on, Kate," says Nan with the slightest indication of a grin.

"Steel door. Like his eyes change from blue to grey and the smile flattens and, though most wouldn't notice, he's done with the situation. He's moved on. No judgement, just done."

Both ladies turn and look at me as if I'm a science experiment.

It's at this point that the houseman comes in and asks if anyone would like a beverage.

"Yes please," I say,"A large, very dry beverage with two olives. The afternoon is just beginning, apparently."

14. Who's for Dinner?

How bad is bad?

"So, what's the something?" I ask.

"I was planning a dinner – about 60 people or so. It was to be another fundraiser – higher stakes this time – towards a new wing at the hospital. It's a fine hospital with wonderful care-givers and we want to help them grow to be the presence they deserve to be."

"Very nice. Very you-and-Walter."

"Oh, this is *all* Walter. He might even come to this! You know how he feels about good health," Nan turns toward Kate,"Our family has had a lot of issues, in case you didn't know, which I'm sure you did."

The Gibsons, in addition to being an enormously successful family with very good hair, are also a famously cursed one, as sometimes happens. Physical and mental illnesses have long been a part of the Gibson legacy, going back generations and continuing to the present day. Their generous support of medical research and facilities has only added to their legend. Walter, especially, has felt it his duty, as a healthy son, to champion and support all things related to health, fitness and research.

"So, what was the Carla question, which now, sadly, no longer matters?"

"Men enjoyed her and she was very good at charming them. She was always a terrific ally in fundraising. Women tended not to like her, understandably, but were usually able to look past her socially, unless, of course, they felt threatened."

Kate interjects,"And by 'threatened', you mean, they thought she was after their man or possibly already had him?"

"Exactly. It happened often enough. She even made a play for Walter once," Nan smiled a knowing smile.

"And what?" asked Kate.

"And nothing," responded Nan. "She didn't realize how ludicrous it was and how ridiculous she looked. Walter loves me."

"He'd be a fool not to."

"That's what I tell him, every chance I get. And I adore him, so, there's that."

"What did you do?"

"I laughed. She got the message. But apparently other women were not so lucky, or were less secure in their marriages, or some combination of the two. And that leads us to Becka Conrad. I don't know her well at all, but she's trying very hard to know me, both here and in New York. We first met at a function for the Met this past year.

"I knew more about her than she thought she knew about me – I wish this new generation would do their homework – anyway, I'd already heard the marriage was, shall we say, chilly?

"Later, after the gala, there were rumblings about Becka's husband and Carla, and I didn't know how much truth there was in that. But Carla loves...loved...a chilly marriage. It was a challenge to her." She turned to Kate and continued,"I despise professional marriages. If you can't share a burger with the guy, take your winnings and move on. That's why I have a soft spot for the mess that was Carla. Agree or disagree, but she knew this strata and she thought these men deserved a little passion. They'd worked hard enough. And if they weren't getting appreciation at home, then she was more than happy to be a cheerleader for one."

Kate is now liking Nan even more, if that's possible, and also melting towards Carla...a little.

Nan continues,"Becka has been lobbying hard to partner in this fundraising venture so I thought I'd ask Able what was what before I unnecessarily ruffled any feathers. A new face, especially a pretty one, can be a blessing in the world of fundraising, so if Becka is sincere, I'd like to know. And if she is, I certainly wouldn't want her to feel set up at our first joint event.

"And perhaps I can persuade you to come, Kate? I have a feeling you'd be a welcome addition anywhere you go. When will you be back in Bucks?"

"I'd love to come! I'm here all the time, right Able? Next weekend in fact."

"Is that right?" I ask with genuine surprise.

"I just decided. You're good with that right? Things are becoming so interesting around here. I don't want to miss anything!"

15. Pleased to Meet You

Won't you guess my name?

Nan met Becka and Victor Conrad at the opening of the Met Costume Exhibit on Rock and Roll Fashion. Nan thought Becka was very fresh and new. Smart, funny, trying a little too hard, but showing great promise. She already knew of Victor through her husband. Walter had said he was on the rise and would be worth knowing. He'd seen him on CNN and followed his career in the Journal, heard he had a pretty wife who did something in the arts. "You should check them out, Nanny. They could be your new pets," he'd said. And so they would be. Nan, in vintage Givenchy, was chatting with friends, holding court, as it were, when Becka approached.

"Mrs. Gibson, I..."

"Please call me Nan. Everyone does. And shall I call you Becka?"

"Yes, please, I...you know my name..."

"Well, then it must be worth knowing." Nan took her by the arm as she continued, "Come, dear, don't faint. Not while wearing Prada. One needs color to wear Prada. There, that's much better. Now, let me tell you a little about yourself. You're charming, perfectly charming, and have a wonderful complexion; you're married to the most exciting young man on Wall Street; you're making quite a name for yourself here at the Met and it's about to become even more resonant since you're being seen talking to me. Let's walk, shall we?"

As they strolled past the Sixties fringe and the Seventies sequins, Nan continued to demonstrate her remarkable skill at small talk while Becka slowly recovered her composure.

"You know, Mrs....Nan, I wasn't expecting you to be so...warm," she regretted the comment as soon as she'd made it.

"No one does, dear. It's one of my secret weapons. Though I must say, Becka, that I wasn't expecting you to be so, well, without fire," she said, still smiling, "I was hoping for more."

Becka rallied to the challenge. "I do apologize for that. I think I left my fire at home this evening. Perhaps it's the outfit. I never feel myself in this shade of green." Nan laughed.

Becka continued, "May we start again? Mrs. Gibson, may I call you Nan? I hear that everyone does. I'm Rebecca Conrad. Please call me Becka."

"I think I shall." Nan smiled, sincerely this time, "Incidentally, I agree with you about the green. Prada in general, in fact, but that's just me."

"No, it's not just you," the voice was low, and the source was very handsome. Ruggedly, romantically, Heathcliff handsome. "Whenever I see Prada I think of PTA meetings and car pools. Oh," he noticed Becka's outfit, "Sorry. Once again wit has conquered grace in the war that is social interaction. I apologize. Feel free to take a cheap shot at my appearance if you'd like," he said with what appeared to be genuine chagrin.

Becka's eyes traveled over him, enjoying the terrain, "Let me see," she said, "so many options."

"Ouch," he replied with a disarming whimper.

"Enough," interrupted Nan. "Shawn, my sweet, I would like you to meet Rebecca Conrad. She has graciously allowed me to call her Becka. You may call her Mrs. Conrad. Becka, this awful excuse for a man is Shawn Patrik, my very best friend and favorite decorating genius."

Becka tried to disguise her excitement. "Call me Becka, please, and it's an honor to meet you, Mr. Patrik. You're reputation precedes you."

"Good God, I hope not," he replied with mock distress. "Oh, you mean the decorating thing. Yes, well..."

"Don't let the little boy act fool you dear, he knows exactly how talented and how much in-demand he is. And how attractive. Now Shawny darling, I'm entrusting you with the well being of our delightful Mrs. Conrad. Trish Davenport is flailing her caftan sleeves at me, presumably to get my attention. Or, perhaps she's having a stroke. Either way she seems to need me, and so I must go. Becka, a pleasure. Let's talk further. I'll phone this week. Shawn, my fallen angel, promise to behave."

"Yes, Nannygoat. Now go, off with you."

Air kisses were exchanged, and Nan, Mrs. Walter Gibson, floated across the room.

Shawn turned his ridiculously large brown eyes to Becka, "Consider yourself blessed, Mrs. Conrad. She likes you."

"And I like her."

"Yes, but that's not as important. Not yet, anyway."

They studied each other knowing they both liked what they saw. "Tell me, Mrs. Conrad... Becka... have you been done?"

"Not in a long time."

He studied her with amusement,"I was referring to your apartment."

She smiled back,"I wasn't."

He paused before responding, "I'd love to see it."

Becka smiled. "I'd love to show it to you."

She had rediscovered her fire. She hadn't left it home after all.

"Becka, you do know I'm gay, yes?"

For the second time that evening she tried to gracefully regain her composure. "And you do know that I'm embarrassed."

She continued in what was hopefully a light, wistful tone, "I suppose I should have guessed."

"Why," he asked, eyebrows arching, "the decorator thing?"

"No," she replied, "because you're handsome and funny."

He chuckled softly, "Why Mrs. Conrad, how you talk." Shawn took her hands in his and said, genuinely, "Friends, then?"

"Yes, please," she said. And after a lovely pause, "You know, I really would love to show it to you...the apartment that is."

"And I would really love to see it...the apartment that is. As for now, I see your glass is empty, and that's something I can take care of to your satisfaction."

Becka laughed. For the first time that evening she was relaxed and enjoying herself. She had made two new friends, and powerful ones at that.

"Well done, Becka," she said to herself. "Well done."

16. Meet Chic/Cute

Nearly perfect.

Victor was on the far side of the exhibit in front of the Jimi Hendrix mannequin, nursing a Manhattan. He had discovered a new definition for boredom. These people – Becka's people. The hard lacquered women who dress up for each other's benefit; the handsome young men who walk them around like show dogs; the actor/model/waiter/busboys who vigorously flirt with both.

She had whined and whined and badgered him into coming – "It's important, Victor. We have to be seen. There are people we need to meet. I was instrumental in pulling this exhibit together. It could mean a great deal to my career. And yours. What about your career, Victor? That's all you really care about anyway, isn't it? Well, isn't it?" Often with Becka it was easier to give in. Just give in. Rollover and play dead. Like she did every night in bed.

"I never would have guessed Hendrix. I'd have thought you were more the Mel Tormé type," the voice was amused and seductive at the same time.

"You would have thought right, much to the dismay of my wife."

"She doesn't know what she's missing then. I'm Carla Montgomery, Mr. Conrad, how do you do?"

She was spectacular. A tall, blonde goddess. Regal, confident, completely at ease. And so sexy. Old fashioned, movie star sexy. She owned this room, or at the very least, all the men in it.

"Much better now, thank you," he replied, "I'm sorry, have we..."

"Met? No. Though I'm well aware of your growing media presence. It's hard to ignore someone so intelligent and attractive – such a rare combination in a man." She smiled a perfect smile.

"Or a woman," he said.

"Oh no, you see it all the time in women. Your wife, for instance. I've heard she's pretty." Somehow she managed to make this last statement sound like a compliment and a condescension.

"Yes, I suppose she is."

"And smart?"

"Cunning. Becka is very cunning."

"Such warm praise from such a loving spouse. Wait, hold still." She reached forward and brushed his right cheek delicately with the ring finger of her left hand. "Eyelash," she said in a husky whisper.

"Are you flirting with me, Ms. Montgomery?" he asked.

"Oh, I think so. Don't you?"

They spoke for a long time. Education, politics, favorite guilty pleasures, favorite books. A real conversation. Part interview, part first date. Of course, Victor came to realize very quickly who she was, much to his embarrassment. They were discussing the recent Matisse exhibit at MoMA when he interrupted his own sentence with, "...Carla Montgomery. You're that Carla Montgomery. The Times, *the books, the champion of American culture Carla Montgomery."*

"In the flesh."

"And lovely flesh it is, too. Please disregard my thick-headedness. You must think I'm an idiot."

"A little humbling is good now and then...but only a very little."

"I enjoy your writing tremendously."

"And I yours. We could learn a lot from each other, Victor," she paused. "It's been wonderful meeting you like this. Do you suppose we could..."

Nan joined their interaction. "Carla, darling, pardon the intrusion. My carriage awaits; and I couldn't possibly leave without saying good night to you and Mr. Conrad, whom I have, in fact, yet to meet. Nan Gibson, Mr. Conrad, how do you do?"

"Very well, thank you." Victor took the extended delicate hand in his own and was stunned by the strength of her grip. Iron fist in a velvet glove, as they say. So this is Nan Gibson, he thought, the queen bee. Becka's role model and favorite icon. Nan this. Nan that. The glamorous Mrs. Gibson. The fabulous Nan. She'd been conjured up one hundred times a day in their home. What would Nan serve for a brunch in mid-October? What

would Nan wear to a chamber music recital? He felt as if he knew her. He felt as if he was married to her. He was sick to death of her, and they'd only just met. She looked as if she knew what he was thinking.

"I've just had the most enchanting conversation with your Becka," she said.

"She must have been thrilled, as of course I am, to meet you." He bowed his head very slightly. Nan smiled the fake, coy smile of a most popular girl in high school, which she surely was.

"Oh Carla, we like our Mr. Conrad, don't we?"

Carla, having never taken her eyes off of him replied clearly, "Yes, we certainly do."

Nan observed them both, then added, again to Carla but eyes focused on Victor, "And I can see he adores you. Despises me, of course, but then the husbands always do, at first. Not to worry, Mr. Conrad, you'll come to appreciate me. It's senseless not to."

In spite of himself, he was being charmed. And she knew it. "Is that a smile, Mr. Conrad? Oh, don't make it so easy. Let me woo you. It's part of the fun."

"It's Victor, please."

"No, not just yet. Give me something to strive for. You're Mr. Conrad. My Mr. Conrad. I think it suits you right now." She gave his chin a playful tap with her beautifully manicured index finger. "And now, children, mother's going home where she's appreciated. Kisses."

She had never stopped smiling and never broken stride. And now she was bidding a royal adieu to the rest of the throng.

"She's amazing, isn't she," said Carla.

"Absolutely," said Victor, rubbing his chin.

"You <u>will</u> like her. Trust me on that," she said, rather sweetly.

"Oh, I already like her," then he turned and looked deeply into her eyes, "and you. Carla, may we continue this, whatever this is, tomorrow over lunch? One o'clock, La Grignotiere?"

"Two o'clock and you've got a date." This could be fun, she thought.

"Two o'clock, then."

17. Do We Like This?

Does it go with the sofa?

On the first Tuesday of every month, I drive into Manhattan to have lunch with Hugo Swann – agent, friend, and the owner/director of The Hugo Swann Gallery in Chelsea. Hugo's a class act. He looks, walks, talks, and dresses like late night coffee and a fine cognac. His eyes are smart and laughing at their own inside joke. His voice is a low, warm rumble. His manners are impeccable, his style smooth. Hugo's a whole lotta something.

We met several years ago, while I was still being represented by the Chesterfield Gallery and Hugo was their Director of Corporate Acquisitions. We liked each other well enough from the start, but rarely crossed paths, usually only at gallery openings. Hugo always had nice things, if a little obscure, to say about my work; and I thought he was impressive, if a little distracted.

Soon after I quit New York and the Chesterfield quit me, Hugo also had a mutual parting of the ways with the gallery. He'd been witness to some shady payment tactics in which the gallery management was profiting, the big name clients were benefitting, and the artists were being cheated out of earnings. When he made his feelings known to his bosses, it was suggested he might be happier elsewhere, perhaps on his own.

And so The Hugo Swann Gallery was born, a few years earlier than he had planned, but such is fate. Hugo called on acquaintances and friends he'd made during his years with the Chesterfield to help him line up financial backing and an artistically impressive frontline. The financing fell into place quickly – Hugo was Hugo, after all. Developing his artistic offering took more time. He wanted to spotlight art that was esthetically more accessible and technically more valid than the usual current fare of silver-plated tchochkes and derivative Ash Can School monstrosities. He sought out what he labeled Abstract Realism – recognizable imagery translated through strong, capable hands into personal expressions of emotion, place, memory, and beauty. Yes, beauty. Imagine.

I was one of the first artists Hugo sought out. He tracked me down and came to visit. I showed him what I'd been up to, he told me his plans – it was professional love at first sight. We've been working together ever since.

On this particular Tuesday, I arrive at the gallery around 1:00. Hugo is schmoozing a young power-couple-in-training. They're trying to decide whether or not they need an enormous pastel drawing of pears by Marguerite Post. It's beautifully done and not cheap at $15,000, but neither of these facts seems to matter. The question is, "Are you sure this is the one our decorator wanted us to see?"

Hugo responds with his usual charm. "Yes, Mrs. Noble. This is the one. Isn't it beautiful? Ms. Vesprey said you, especially, would appreciate the delicacy, the nuance of the artist's hand, being such a delicate beauty yourself; and you, Mr. Noble, would appreciate the value of an artist who's prices have tripled in the last ten months."

At this last statement, the young Mr. Noble actually stops scrolling and looks up from his phone.

Hugo continues, "Miss Vesprey certainly knows her clients, I can see that. Why don't I leave you with your drawing for a moment. If you'll excuse me."

He strolls across the large open room to greet me.

"Genius," he says, "good to see you. You're looking well."

"Thanks, boss. Not too shabby yourself. Listen, don't let me interrupt."

Hugo looks back at the couple, who have no idea what they're looking at or what they're supposed to do next.

"I'm closing a sale. You want to help?"

"Sure."

"How'd you like to play famous artist for a few minutes, and let me introduce you? I'll buy you lunch?"

"You were already buying me lunch."

As we walk towards the young couple, I ask, "So, who are Barbie and Ken, anyway, and what are they interested in?"

"Their names are Tim and Mallory Noble, and they're interested in themselves. But they're looking at a Marguerite Post pastel piece."

"Love her. Okay, *Famous Artist* at your service."

I do my bit for art and commerce, performing my role with conviction and the right amount of attitude. Hugo continues to coax them with his charm. Half an hour later the drawing has been purchased; and the proud, new owners are gone, having been rescued from their obvious lack of ease by the overwhelming Ms. Vesprey.

Eleanor Vesprey, all gestures and enthusiasm, is a grande dame of interior design. She created her signature look of Versailles-inspired grandeur and golden excess in the late seventies and has never strayed from the formula. She is the only choice for a certain type of client – one who believes Marie Antoinette had the right idea. Her fashion sense – also delineated in the late seventies, also unchanged since then – is severely elegant and restrained. Chanel for daytime, Dior for evening, in black, grey or beige; good jewelry – big on bracelets, and handmade shoes from a little shop in Rome. She wears her dark brown hair in a classic pageboy, occasionally pulled back with Audrey Hepburn sunglasses or a black, grosgrain ribbon. Whippet-thin and melodramatically poised, she speaks with a finishing school attentiveness to enunciation and the metaphorical meanderings common to her profession.

"The pears! My darlings, the fruit of Aphrodite! And pastel...PASTEL! So difficult yet so masterfully done...shhh...soft. Like Brahms. Listen, do you hear it? Our space will be filled to overflowing with Jongkind, Sisley and the rest of the old boys and then...a bit of whimsy...modern poetry...our pears for the breakfast room! Such fun! Come, my darlings, there's an Aubusson across town that will positively BE our library! Hugo! Lovely. And Mr. Ryder, I've got my eye on you." And with that, they were gone.

"She's a trip," I say, "but tell me something. How do two kids like that get to work with the great and powerful Eleanor Vesprey?"

"How do you think? Money, connections, and VIP's – Very Important Parents," Hugo flips through a copy of *Town and Country* sitting on his desk and points to a photograph of a meticulously manicured couple of indeterminate age.

"Ah," I recognize the parents immediately, "Some people have all the luck."

"At least all the money. And thanks to Miss Vesprey, some of that money flows this way... So, famous artist, you hungry?"

"I could eat. Where are we going?"

"*Buddy's*?"

"Perfect."

"*Buddy's* it is then."

18. You Want Fries with That?

More than the usual.

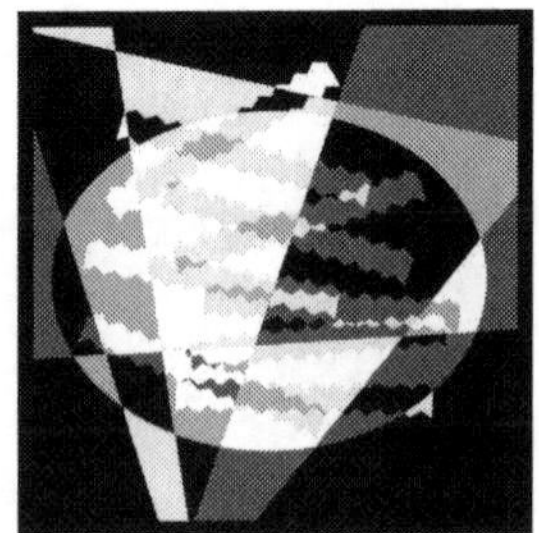

The front room at *Buddy's* still has the original Mahogany bar and black and white tile floor from the turn of the last century. The lighting is dim, the juke box selection is jazz only. Booths along the wall are high-backed and private, ideal for business discussions or romantic assignations. It's also just a great place to hang, with friendly service, generous drinks and good, uncomplicated New York bar food.

Hugo leads the way to his usual booth, the fourth one in from the door. We get comfortable, order beers, burgers and fries, and commence our very relaxed, bi-weekly business meeting. By the time food comes, business is completed and the discussion turns to Carla Montgomery.

"Horrible, isn't it?" I say.

"Hard to believe. They're saying now that she knew whoever did it. No struggle, opened door, lights on, all that," Hugo pauses. "I'm sorry, is this too weird to talk about?"

"No, don't worry about it. That was ancient history. We got together a couple of times, then just like that, it was over."

"You mean, as soon as the Chesterfield dropped you."

"Yeah, well, there was that. I wasn't appropriate to be seen with anymore. Artist non gratis. Funny thing is, though, I didn't hate her for it. You couldn't. She was a bitch a lot of the time, but she was honest. And sexy? Unbelievable!"

"Well, let's say men couldn't hate her," Hugo says between swallows, "I can't think of one woman who didn't."

"True enough. So, you think a woman killed her?"

"Lots of women had the right."

"I've got a strong left myself," the sharp, clear voice of Kate Lindsey breaks into our conversation. "What are we talking about? Move over, handsome. I want to sit next to the sexiest man in New York," she says as she slides in next to Hugo, who cups her chin and gives her a quick kiss.

"Hello, lovely lady," he says.

"Let me interrupt this tender moment," I say. "What's this 'sexiest man in New York' thing? I thought that was me."

"Oh, it was you, bunky. But then you moved. Now you're the sexiest man in Pennsylvania," she says, stealing a fry from Hugo's plate.

"Quick save, though it doesn't have the same ring, does it... 'sexiest man in Pennsylvania'..."

"Lotta cute farm boys in Pennsylvania," she replies in a sing-song voice, "and landscapers with those muscular forearms, and truckers, let's not forget the truckers..."

"This could take a while, Hugo. Kate's having a moment. Mind if I interrupt your reverie? What brings you to *Buddy's* in the middle of a work day? Are you following us?"

"A birthday lunch for one of the account execs. Sharon King. Says she's 36. She's really 44." She steals another fry. "I thought I might see you. Hugo and I run into each other here all the time, don't we Hugo?"

"Shhh. I thought that was our secret," he says with great earnestness. "Able, the truth is we're having an affair."

"Yes, it's true. *L'affaire du pomme de terre*," Kate adds in her best mini-series French.

"An affair of the potato?"

"You gotta admit, their french fries are good. Honestly, it's the only decent restaurant in the neighborhood for lunch. I run into everyone I know here at *Buddy's*. But enough about illicit affairs and grand obsessions. What were you two talking about?"

"Illicit affairs and grand obsessions," responds Hugo.

"Oh?" says Kate.

"Carla Montgomery," say I.

"Oh," says Kate disdainfully.

"Hugo was saying that all women hated her, and I was saying that all men loved her."

"Case in point," she interjects, pointing a floppy french fry in my direction. "Well, I agree with Hugo. I only met her once or twice, but she was the kind of woman other women despise. You see, gentlemen, smart women hate to see smart men turned into simpering wimps by a conniving bitch."

"One mustn't speak ill of the dead."

"That was the nicest thing I could think of to say. She was a user, simply put...and more beautiful than she had a right to be. There. My new best friend, Nan Gibson, has softened my opinion the tiniest little bit."

"You gotta admit, she was smart, too," I say.

"Oh, she was brilliant," says Kate.

"And a good writer," says Hugo.

"I wouldn't go that far," says Kate.

"I think I'm with Kate on that one. Her writing was a little too self-important for me. She knew her stuff, no doubt about it, but Carla was no Robert Hughes."

"Or Sister Wendy," says Kate with a smirk, "Too many bad habits."

And pause.... "However," I continue,"she had a great mind for business and trends...like Madonna used to, to keep with the religious imagery."

"Very true," says Hugo. "She's responsible for putting a lot of creative people on the map. And not just fine artists. Musicians, fashion people, architects. Carla made a lot of careers."

"And destroyed just as many," says Kate definitively. "Personally, I think she was killed by a whole bunch of people. A *Murder on the Orient Express* type of thing. All the artists she dropped when she was bored, all the wives of the husbands she stole..."

"Interesting idea," says Hugo, "but they do know it was one person. The neighbor who discovered her body returned from walking her dog just in time to see someone step away from the body and head for the fire exit. She couldn't tell if it was a man or a woman."

"That's one of the problems with New York," Kate says while reapplying her lipstick. "You often can't tell if it's a man or a woman." She smacks her lips together, closes her compact and drops it in her smart little Kate Spade bag. "It makes dating so...problematic."

She slides out of the booth. "Boys, I hate to leave you, but I should get back. Hugo, my love, I only have fries for you."

He laughs. "Good to see you, Kate"

"Able, I'll see you tonight?" Kate had invited me to be her date for a benefit at the Plaza honoring women in advertising.

"Eight o'clock, right? Why don't I meet you at the bar in the St. Regis for a pre-benefit cocktail. Shall we say seven-ish?"

"Absolutely-ish! I'll see you then."

She kisses me on the cheek and heads for the door, waving back over her shoulder as she goes. Hugo and I sit back and watch her make her exit.

"You gotta love her," says Hugo.

"Yes, you do. She wouldn't have it any other way."

19. Beauty is Its Own Reward

How big is big?

The painting is huge, six feet wide by eight feet tall, an abstract expression of size if nothing else. Mostly black with a thick cement-like texture, a thin line drawing of a cube is scraped into the surface at the top left. A valentine from the 1950's, a bright pink heart inscribed with the sentiment *Be Mine*, has been glued to the lower right corner.

Leo Ventura faces the canvas and studies it for several minutes. He grabs a butcher knife off of his work table and attacks the painting, stabbing it again and again, ripping through the canvas leaving large, gaping holes. In thirty seconds he's done. His art is complete. Leo drops the knife, lights a cigarette and steps back to view his newest creation.

He falls into the beat-up, paint-spattered wingback chair, the only chair in his painting studio, and exhales slowly, enjoying the vision of the smoke obscuring his work. "There, Carla," he thinks to himself, "this one's for you." He exhales again and puts the cigarette out in the overflowing ashtray on the floor.

Leo walks across the room and stands in front of a full length mirror leaning against a metal book case. He studies his reflection. What had she called him – "One of Carravagio's boys"? Whatever.

The description fits. Leo has an overripe look about him; something good going bad. He's young, only 22, with the hard-muscled body of a wrestler...or a street thug – smooth, olive skin; wiry, animal grace; a funky I-just-got-laid kind of walk.

From the neck up he's a little bit of heaven...or somewhere farther south – thick, black, curly hair; dark, brown eyes looking out under stupidly long lashes; a small nose, almost pretty; and a mouth so full, so sensuous, it's practically obscene. It's the Dick Tracy jawline and bull neck that add to the rock star androgyny everyone finds so enticing. Carla *Montgomery was right*, he thinks. *I am a Carravagio boy; The Dirty Bacchus. Come and get it, if you can.*

Leo looks at his mouth, his shoulders, his broad chest and perfect abs. He picks up a can of black paint sitting open on the floor, and flings it at the mirror. As the paint runs down the mirror's surface, Leo watches himself disappear.

"What happens to me now, Carla?" he says out loud, "What happens t

The first time he met Carla Montgomery, Leo Ventura was serving her caviar. It w. Shawn Patrik's annual Sweet 16 birthday party, with seventy of the decorator's nearest a. dearest in attendance. Carla was one of the seventy. Leo was one of the catering crew.

He was still a senior in college – Cooper Union – where he was studying painting. He'd worked the catering circuit since his sophomore year, to help pay for school. This was the first party he'd done for Silver Spoon, *though. They were the best caterers in New York, with the best clientele. He was a little nervous about it. Leo knew it was a great way to make connections for his future career in art. Bobby Tyler had said as much.*

Bobby Tyler, the celebrated new talent on the abstract art scene, as well as Leo's favorite teacher, had arranged this gig for him, and he didn't want to let him down. Mr. Tyler told him to put his natural charms and lush looks to good use. He already knew how Leo was using them to supplement his income, and this party circuit had a much better clientele for that business, too.

Actually it was one of his other teachers who started him down that other road. She was Margo Davies, a short, pinched, expressionless figure painter who taught life drawing – funny, that. Miss Davies favored bulky sweaters, even in the summer, and round glasses with thick, black frames. She wore her dull, brown hair pulled back in a sloppy bun; she always carried an unlit cigarette, which she fingered anxiously. She was a mess. Good teacher, though. Good artist, too.

One day after class, Miss Davies asked Leo if he would consider posing for her. She was working on a series of allegorical pieces for her next gallery show and thought he would be perfect to represent Wanton Youth. *Of course he would be paid, she said, but he'd have to pose nude. Would that be a problem?*

No big deal, Leo thought.

Miss Davies asked him to come to her studio in the East Village the following evening. Leo showed up around 7:00. She answered the door wearing a tight, white T-shirt, no bra, and green drawstring doctor's pants. No glasses. No bun. No sweater. No shit. Margo Davies was a babe, how about that?

She said, "Hello, thanks for coming." and led him into her studio, where she proceeded to show him sketches for the painting in progress. Taped to the wall over her work table was a large pieced together drawing which represented the entire composition. Three figures stood in stylized classical poses; the setting appeared to be Central Park with midtown Manhattan in the background. She told him the figures symbolized Idle Youth, Industrious Youth, *and* Poetic Youth. *He recognized them as his classmates Signe, Jake, and Catherine, each carefully draped to hide their nakedness. On the right side of the g was a large vacant spot with the words LEO and WANTON scribbled in.*

The sketch was impressive. Strong. Confident. There was no doubting Miss Davies' talent. Leo had already gotten a lot out of her class, in spite of her lack of enthusiasm about practically everything. But now, especially after seeing her on her home turf, he was honored to be in a Margo Davies painting.

She offered him a glass of wine to relax and showed him where she wanted him to stand.

"Do you want me to strip now?" Leo asked.

"Sure," she replied returning to her easel and flipping back the cover on a large drawing pad.

He kicked off his boots, yanked off his T-shirt and dropped his khakis. That was it. Five seconds tops.

She looked up nonchalantly from her drawing pad, eyeing him up and down, pausing briefly below his waist. Her facial expression indicated nothing; her nipples pushing against the thin fabric of her T-shirt told another story.

"Nice, Leo," she said clinically, "your body is as beautiful as I'd expected. Now, what I'd like you to do...do you mind if I show you?" She returned to where he was standing and removed the glass of wine from his hand. She bent down and set it on the floor. She moved his feet apart slightly and asked him to center his weight. As she stood, she supported herself with one hand on each of Leo's thighs, squeezing gently. She slid her hands up to his hips, then moved them smoothly behind him and cupped his rock hard ass, tilting his pelvis forward. She glanced down at Leo's growing pleasure.

A little nervous, a little confused, he said, "I think my price just went up."

"That's not all," she said smiling, "We agreed on $100.00 for posing. I'll give you another hundred for sex."

"I was kidding," he said quickly. Then, "You're gonna pay me a hundred bucks just to have sex with you?"

"From what I can see, I'd be getting a lot of value for the money."

Leo let out a short breath, "You're a trip, Miss Davies."

"You know, Leo," she removed her T-shirt, "I think at this point," she pulled the drawstring, letting her pants fall to the floor, "you might want to call me Margo."

After their first session, Leo continued to pose for Margo, and sleep with her until her painting was completed. He learned a lot...about a lot of things. He asked her to spread the word among her fellow artists and teachers about his modeling capabilities, which she did enthusiastically. As a result, Leo was kept very busy...and received many A's for his efforts.

He made sure it was clear he was totally straight...but flexible. Equal opportunity and all that. He developed quite a fan club among the middle-aged and advancing middle-aged artistic community. The women, for the most part, were adventurous and surprisingly aggressive. The men, on the other hand, were usually gentle but strong, and very, very good with their hands. Usually Leo could tell who was interested in him for, well, for whatever. Sometimes not, but usually. It was the call from Mr. Tyler, though, that he was completely unprepared for.

At 28, Bob Tyler was the youngest member of the faculty, teaching Advanced Painting and Abstract Theory. *He was big, 6'2", with a soap opera face and short, blond, lifeguard hair. He worked out and had the body to show for it. The female students, all of them, had a crush on him; and the male students, all of them, wanted to be just like him. As for Leo, it never occurred to him that, well...Mr. Tyler just didn't seem...but he guessed he'd find out that following Tuesday night.*

Bob Tyler's painting career was taking off like a comet. His name and face were always popping up in the media; his press agent was working overtime, clearly. His last show got a notable review in Art News, Vanity Fair *did a small piece naming names from his impressive list of collectors, and* Architectural Digest *just photographed his loft in Tribeca. He was a regular on* Radar *and* TMZ. *Not bad for 28.*

On that following Tuesday, Leo stood outside the loft building, formerly a textile warehouse and now home to three artists, two young movie stars, several brokers, and a couple of trust fund babies. He buzzed the buzzer marked 5. He heard Mr. Tyler's voice say, "Come on up. Fifth floor." As in the whole fifth floor. Leo took the short elevator ride and stepped out directly into Mr. Tyler's loft; minimal with poured concrete floors and slick mid-century modern furniture, large demi-lune windows and soaring ceilings.

"Leo! Come on in." He heard his voice before he saw him. "Turn left at James Dean. I'm working in back."

Leo saw a life-sized cut-out figure of the actor, a lobby card from one of his old movies, twenty feet or so across the room. He headed in that direction and turned left. A half a city block away, but still in the same loft, he saw Mr. Tyler.

"There you are, Leo. Good to see you. Need anything? Beer? Water? Soda?" He was crouched over an enormous un-stretched canvas, spreading yellow paint around with a mop – bare feet, bare chest, wearing only a pair of jeans.

"Water'd be good," Leo responded quietly.

"Great. Don't mind helping yourself, do you? The kitchen's back there," he nodded over his left shoulder, "and could you get me one, too? I'm just about done here for tonight.

Just need a few more minutes."

"No problem," Leo headed back to the slick, stainless steel kitchen with the Sub-Zero fridge and the Wolf range, standard issue for New Yorkers who don't cook. When he returned with the two bottles of Evian, Mr. Tyler was putting down his mop and stretching out his back muscles.

Leo handed him the bottled water.

"Thanks, hot shot. Cheers," he smiled and took a big gulp. "So," again he swallowed, "what do I get for a hundred bucks?"

"Well, uh," Leo was caught off guard. "Well, first off, I'm straight, but ..."

"Yeah?" Mr. Tyler interrupted with one eyebrow halfway up his forehead, "Me too," again he smiled that smile, "Variety's always nice, though, don't you think?"

He stepped over to Leo and put his arm around him, pulling him in close. He brought his mouth up to Leo's ear and whispered, "Relax. That's not what I asked you here for."

Leo felt his face becoming flushed.

"You look disappointed," his teacher continued, "that's nice..."

Leo knew he was turning a brighter shade of red.

Mr. Tyler continued, "...no, I just wanted to talk," he watched Leo, smiling all the while. "Look, I seem to be making you uncomfortable. Let me go put a shirt on."

"No, no, that's o.k. It's just, well, you're hot!"

Mr. Tyler laughed. "Why don't we go into the living room. I've seen enough paint for one night."

He ushered Leo back past James Dean and over to the two low slung, red leather sofas.

"First off, my friends call me Bobby; and I think you and I are going to be good friends."

"I'd like that."

"I'm glad," His eyes navigated all of Leo. "You really are something to see."

"Um, thanks," Leo said coyly, "you too."

Bobby pulled his feet up onto the couch and crossed his legs yoga style. "It's my inheritance. You should see my parents. Anyway...I wanted to talk to you about your future," he took one last swallow from his water bottle and set it on the floor. "You're a good painter, Leo, probably the best in my class."

"Really?"

"Yep. You're smart, you work hard, you take chances, and if talent were enough, your career would be a sure thing. Unfortunately, talent's only about 10%, if that, of what it takes to make it as an artist these days."

"Look where you've gotten with your talent."

"I'm proud of my work, don't get me wrong. Very proud. Downright conceited, as a matter of fact. But what jump started my career was good teeth, broad shoulders and a brain.

"The bottom line is this – the art world is controlled and orchestrated by a few hundred people, max. They decide who gets a show, who's gonna be famous, who's gonna be the next big thing; and if you're smart, which you are, and willing to play, you can do very well. If you don't play, you'll spend the rest of your life knocking on doors that'll never open to you, no matter how talented you are."

"Sounds like a game show," Leo said, smirking.

"It is, or can be. It can be exciting and rewarding, too. Look, it all depends on what you want. If it's just about the creative process for you, then let's stop talking and go get some food. But if you want more, and I think you do, if you want the name and the fame and the money and the place in history, this is how it works.

"The group that decides everything is made up mostly of influential men, mostly gay or bi, and society women with too much money and too much free time. Occasionally you get a powerful straight guy, like Alan Fleming, who really knows his art and is genuinely interested in supporting talent; or a brilliant and sensitive woman, like Megan Hewitt, who wants to be this generation's Peggy Guggenheim. But for the most part, it's the big deal interior decorators who will talk you up to their clients, or the society dames whose husbands have told them to go buy something important, as long as it'll improve in value, and these ladies and gents would love for that to be yours, if only you'd sleep with them, you big, dangerous artist, you."

Leo started to laugh.

"Sounds funny, I know, but it's true. I used to be a cater-waiter for Silver Spoon, you've heard of them? They do all the charity benefits and high-end private parties. This one night – I was still a senior in college – we were doing a big deal for the deKooning retrospective at the Whitney. I was serving pigs in blankets to pigs in tuxedoes, and this woman kept waving me over. I didn't know her name, but her face was very familiar. She was in her forties or fifties somewhere – with that crowd it's hard to tell.

"She asked me my name, and I told her. She asked what I did when I wasn't carrying a

silver tray. I said I was an artist. She squeezed my bicep and said she knew I had to be something in the arts because I was so beautiful. I said thank you and tried to explain that I had to get back to work. She said she thought she could help advance my artistic career and wasn't that better than being a party favor. Then she introduced herself as Trish Davenport, as in Mrs. James Davenport, as in The Davenport Fellowship, The Davenport Collection, The Davenport Wing of Contemporary American Art at the...."

"Oh!" said Leo, genuinely impressed.

"Exactly." Bobby continued, "She said she'd love to see my work. Maybe she could come to my studio, or I could come to her home. Wednesday. Lunch. Bring my slides. We'd talk. What a break, right? Mrs. James Davenport wanted to see my work! Well, she wanted to see something, but it wasn't my work.

"I went to her house – embassy is more like it. One of those great old buildings on the Upper East Side between Madison and Park, filled with major antique furniture – Cleopatra's chairs, Napoleon's tables, Henry VIII's spittoons, for Christ's sake! And the art collection's unbelievable – Pollock, Johns, Rauschenberg, Agnes Martin, Rothko... everybody!

"A butler led me up the huge curving staircase in the foyer, passing a series of Matisse cutouts as we went – ya know, I'm convinced that Matisse is still alive and churning out those cut-outs somewhere in Queens. They keep popping up. Anyway, he took me to the second floor sitting room, as opposed to the first and third floor sitting rooms, I guess, asked me to wait, and said, 'Madam will be with you shortly.' A half an hour later Mrs. Davenport came in, walked over to me, took my right hand in both of hers and kissed me on the mouth, hard. Then she stepped back and smiled at me kind of funny. She looked a little older in daylight but prettier, too. Not so harsh.

"She said she wanted to be my benefactress, my Medici. I said she hadn't even seen my work yet. She said that didn't really matter, she was sure I was very talented. She reached forward and unzipped my jeans. Then she pulled junior out to play. I couldn't believe it. I didn't know what to do. The whole time, she spoke in a calm, casual tone about my up and coming first show, and how she'd already brought me up with the Bentley-Shiff Gallery, all she had to do was call and confirm it, and how she was going to plan an unveiling cocktail party for the two new pieces she was commissioning.

"My head was spinning, and she was still stroking me, and I was confused. Then she stopped, ripped my shirt open and started biting my chest. I grabbed her wrists and pulled her hands away and said, 'Mrs. Davenport, I don't think we should be doing this.' And she looked at me, cool as anything, and said, 'Do you want to be famous, or don't you? You're pretty, but there are others just as pretty. And I need a project. So what's it going to be, Mr. Tyler, do you want me to make you the next Picasso, or will it be someone else?' She turned and walked back across the room, then said, in her best uptown hostess voice, 'I wish you well in your painting career. If you'd like to continue this conversation, I'll be upstairs in my bedroom. Oh, and do try not to take too long deciding. I've a manicure appointment at 3:00.'

"So, there I stood with my dick hanging out and my shirt ripped open. And I figured, what the fuck," Bobby stretched and spread out on the couch.

"So?" asked Leo.

Bobby looked around the room and said, "I live here, don't I? And my paintings sell before they're dry. And I'm the, what is it, 'the bright, new star in the art universe,' or so says Carla Montgomery. Yes, I did the deed with Trish Davenport and had a good time doing it – she can be pretty creative. And she was good for her word, let me tell you. She got me hooked up with the right people and told me who to be especially nice to, if you know what I mean, and I'm sure that you do."

"I don't know what to say," said Leo.

"Look," Bobby replied, "I'm being straight with you because, like I said, I like you, Leo, and I think you're the real deal.

"Now, some people would think this was crap, that I'm a hustler, plain and simple, so I'd appreciate it if this conversation was just between you and me; but the way I look at it, it's business, nothing more, nothing less. I like sex and I'm good at it. I like to paint, and I'm good at that. The one helps me to do the other on a grander scale. Nobody gets hurt, and everybody's happy. It would be nice if talent were enough, but it's not.

"You're hot, Leo, and you know it. And good looks open a lot of doors. Believe me, I know I'm handsome. I've always been handsome. But I didn't have anything to do with it, so it's no brag, just fact. Like you. You're a knockout. Lucky, lucky you. So, why not use what you've got? You've been giving it away for a hundred bucks a pop to a bunch of never-will-be's and never-were's. I think it's time you moved up to the big league."

"I hear what you're saying, but I don't know any of those people."

"But you know me. And I'm still friends with the guys at Silver Spoon. *You're still doing the catering thing, right?"*

"Yeah, with The Food Company.*"*

"Good. Well, Silver Spoon *has a better clientele. My buddy Jack, who's one of the owners, told me he needs new waiters; and he's looking for hot, young guys with a little experience under their belts, no pun intended. That would be you. Once you're in there, things will start happening. I could introduce you directly to some of the powers that be, but, trust me, this way's better. That crowd likes to 'discover' new talent. It makes them feel creative. That way they can take credit for every success you ever have."*

"Yeah, and what if I fail?"

"If you fail, you fail. They'll forget they ever knew you and move on to the next." He walked over to a desk by the windows and wrote down the phone number for Silver Spoon. *He came back to where Leo was still sitting and handed him the piece of paper*

with the number on it. "And believe me, there's always a new one. But right now, it's you. Give Jack a call tomorrow afternoon. I'll speak with him in the morning and tell him you'll be in touch. Now, you hungry? How about Chinese?"

"That's it? You really don't want to..."

"Friends, Leo. Remember?"

"Yeah," Leo smiled. "Cool."

Leo made the call and was hired sight unseen on Bobby Tyler's recommendation. His first job would be the birthday party for Shawn Patrik, the society decorator. This was apparently an annual event, a Sweet 16 Birthday Party, that the decorator threw for himself. The guest list was high-octane; seventy of the city's biggest names in business, fashion, society and the arts. Shawn knew everybody and everybody knew Shawn. Now, Shawn would also know Leo Ventura.

Shawn was still in his robe, getting ready for the evening, when the catering crew arrived. He knew them all, having hired Silver Spoon for more than a few events over the last several years, and always enjoyed kidding around with his favorites. They were college kids, mostly, and actors and dancers. And they were always cute and so eager to please. Like puppies. Perky, little downtown puppies with bright eyes, and shiny coats, and waggly, little tails.

Jack asked if they could go over a few last minute details when, over Jack's shoulder, Shawn spotted Leo for the first time.

"I think my heart just stopped. I'm sorry, Jack, were you saying something?"

Jack looked back in the direction of Shawn's gaze. "Ah", he said. He called back toward the bar, "Leo. Could you come here, please? I'd like you to meet your boss for tonight."

Leo set the tray of glasses down in front of him and came over to join the two men.

"Hi," he said, extending his hand, "I'm Leo Ventura."

"Yes, you certainly are," said Shawn. Just like puppies, he thought. "I'm Shawn. Shawn Patrik. Welcome to my humble home. And thank you for being a part of my celebration. It feels more festive already."

Jack interrupted, "Leo, I think Jimmy needs a hand with the champagne."

"Sure thing. Nice meeting you, sir," he started to turn away, then turned back, "Oh, and happy birthday."

Shawn let out an audible sigh as he watched Leo return to the bar.

"Jack, you always know just what to get me for my birthday."

"Sorry to disappoint you."

"Then he must be dessert. I'd certainly like to..."

"Shawn, he's 21."

"And your point would be?"

"My point would be that you're ... not 21."

Shawn cut his eyes at his friend, "That's right. Tonight I'm 16. Sweet 16."

"There's nothing sweet about you, Shawn I think I'd better go warn the kid."

"Good idea. And while you're at it, could you ask him to bring me a dressing drink?" Shawn stepped back to his bedroom door, then turned with a flourish. "I shall be in the master bath, finishing my ablutions."

Jack chuckled and shook his head, "Very Loretta Young," he said.

"Thank you for noticing."

Leo brought Shawn his drink, a Silver Bullet in a very large glass – lots of vodka, a few drops of scotch and a little twist of lemon – Shawn had already finished dressing and was wearing a black cashmere v-neck sweater, black jeans, a black belt with a silver buckle and a silver Cartier tank watch. No shoes. No socks. Standing in front of a massive Baroque framed mirror, combing his hair, Shawn saw Leo's reflection waiting at the bedroom door.

Leo spoke first. "Your drink, sir."

"Sir?" Shawn looked off in the distance contemplatively, "Sir. I think I like that." He turned to face Leo and took his cocktail from the tray. "Here's to you, Leo Ventura," he said,"Bottom's up, just the way I like it."

Leo laughed in spite of himself.

"So, what do you think, Leo Ventura? How do I look?"

"Very handsome, sir."

"Not bad for an old man, right? Must be all this damned clean living." He downed a quarter of his drink. "Tell me, Leo Ventura, what do you do, when you're not serving up liquid and visual refreshment? Actor slash model? Trade show spokesperson? Rent boy?"

Leo looked down at his tray, "I'm studying to be an artist, sir."

"Are you any good?"

"Well, I've still got a lot to ..."

"Cut. Delete. Wrong answer." Shawn looked at the younger man affectionately. "When someone like me asks someone like you if you're good at what you do, you say, 'Yes. Very,' without hesitation. Talented people like to know other talented people. Hesitation only attracts wimps. They may admire your modesty, but they can't do shit for your career."

"Excuse me, Shawn," it was Jack at the bedroom door, "Your guests are arriving, and I could use Leo out here."

"I'm sure we could all use Leo Ventura somewhere." Shawn smiled at the younger man, then he looked to his old friend at the door. "We'll be right out. And don't worry, Jack, we're not breaking any laws in here."

Jack shook his head with a bemused expression, then returned to his post in the kitchen. Shawn killed the rest of his drink and handed the empty glass to Leo.

"Come on, Leo Ventura. It's show time. Now remember what I said," he reached forward and straightened Leo's bow tie. "You're going to meet a lot of heavy hitters tonight. Enjoy it. Because they're going to want to know you. For them, you're like a gift from Cartier. It doesn't really matter what's inside, it's the box that gets them excited. And baby boy," he patted Leo's ass, "you've got a real nice little package there, gift-wrapped and everything."

They returned to the livingroom where a dozen people had already made themselves at home. Nina Simone was singing on the sound system; the lights had been turned down a notch or two to soften the effects of aging and alcohol. Someone told a joke, and light laughter floated through the room. The stage was set, and what a stage it was...

Shawn's home was his calling card. It was in the heart of Chelsea, a part of Manhattan some people call the new Soho, for all of the art galleries, and other people call Boystown, for obvious reasons. Shawn's apartment had originally been two separate apartments that he combined into one. He gutted them and reconfigured the space so as to make the most of a spectacular downtown view. Tumbled limestone floors had been installed throughout. The lighting and sound systems were worthy of Lincoln Center. As to the actual furnishings, how can they be described? Eclectic? To be sure. Theatrical? Unabashedly. Luxurious? Without a doubt.

Part of Shawn's success came from his ability to create fantasies for his clients; movie sets for the dramas that were their lives. He envisioned the surroundings these fascinating people so richly deserved, or so he said. And so they believed.

The theme for his own apartment was "Cary Grant circa 1950 meets Queen Elizabeth I in North Africa...in the fog." And it was, somehow, all of that.

The party was building beautifully. Financiers chatted with personal trainers, models flirted with doctors. Here an artist. There a broker. And everywhere, the witty and charismatic host kept things light and floating along. It was two hours into the evening when Shawn was embraced from behind and serenaded with "Happy birthday, Mr. Decorator," sung in a breathy Marilyn whisper.

"Ah, the late Carla Montgomery," he said jokingly.

"If I wasn't always late, how would you know it was me?" She spun him around and gave him a big hug and kiss. "Happy Birthday, sweetie!"

"Thanks, beauty. Come," he said, twirling his index finger, indicating that Carla should pirouette, "Let's have a look."

She was wearing black slacks, a black cashmere v-neck sweater, a black belt with a silver buckle, and very high, black Roger Vivier pumps.

"Gucci?" he asked. She nodded. "Very nice," he said, 'O.k., my turn." With that, Shawn did his own spin.

"Gucci?" she asked. He nodded.

"Very nice," she replied.

They laughed.

"We do have such good taste, don't we?" said Shawn. "So, are you stag tonight, or did you bring one of your many admirers? Victor Conrad, perhaps?"

"Shhh! Not so loud. Besides, I have no idea what you're talking about," she said, as she exaggeratedly fluffed her hair.

"That's right! He's married! What was I thinking?" he said teasingly. "Incidentally, the wife suspects."

Shawn was in the midst of redecorating Becka and Victor Conrad's country place and had ingratiated himself to both of them. He was Becka's mentor and confidant, as well as being Victor's handball partner and new friend. He talked them into and then helped them purchase a country place in Bucks County, very near his own. Naturally he'd be renovating and decorating the place for them. They both told him much more than they should have, regarding the state of their marriage, suspected infidelities and such, mistakenly believing his soulful, concerned expression implied discretion. That would have been wrong.

Of course, Shawn already knew all about Victor's affair with Carla from Carla herself. Shawn and Carla told each other everything. They'd been pals for years, helping each other into and out of many an awkward romantic escapade. Carla said she and Shawn were Night-stalkers. He said they were a couple of cheap sluts covering their butts.

Shawn continued, "Victor, of course, has told me all of the lurid details – I especially liked the elevator incident – and, honey, my little peach tart, the man's in love with you. Head over fucking heels."

"I know," Carla said distractedly.

"And Becka... well, she hates you anyway because you are, after all, you. But, she does suspect. Apparently Nan slipped up recently and said she'd run into both you and Victor at Hugo Swann's gallery, and wasn't that a coincidence?"

"Well, it could have been."

"I don't think so. Neither did Becka. Victor couldn't care less about galleries."

"He's learning to. I'm teaching him."

"Victor would sing in a karaoke bar if he thought it would make you happy."

"Victor Conrad in a karaoke bar. Funny." Carla smiled to herself, conjuring up the image of Victor's performance. "Well, Becka couldn't care less about Victor, so I don't think there's any problem, really."

"Oh, she doesn't care for Victor at all. Despises him, in fact. But she vehemently defends the shrine of Victor and Becka Conrad. The Couple. The Image. And no one, especially some oversexed, overeducated hussy from Philadelphia is gonna screw that up."

"I love it when you call me 'hussy'."

He brought his mouth to her ear, "Hussy," he hissed.

She giggled, "To be perfectly honest, and this is just between you and me, Sugar, and I mean that, o.k.?"

"O.k."

"I think Mr. Conrad is on his way out. I'm getting bored."

"Already?"

"I know, I know, I'm horrible. Barely human. What can I say. It's just that, I don't know, he's gotten so moony. At first I thought it was sweet, but now it's just annoying. What's a girl to do? My Master of the Universe has turned into Poindexter at the Prom."

Shawn put his arm around his pouting friend's shoulder. "Well, I'm disappointed," he said, "I thought you two were the perfect illicit couple. So Waspy, so rich, so attractive. And he is attractive, don't you think? I've seen him in the locker room at the tennis club, and he's certainly got all the right equipment. I'd do 'im."

"Sweetie, you'd do just about anyone...and have, come to think of it." She paused, rolling her diamond tennis bracelet around her wrist. "However, truth be told, Victor isn't great in bed. Not for me, anyway. He's a giver, and you know how I hate that. So respectful, so sensitive – spare me."

"Sounds like heaven. A sweet, little boy in a four thousand dollar suit. Mind if I have a shot?"

"Be my guest. You've always been good to the needy."

"Just call me St. Patrik."

Carla giggled. "What I need in my life right now, besides you of course, is a little muscle. A little danger. A few rough edges."

As if on cue, Leo appeared, offering a silver tray to the two of them. "Caviar?" he asked. Carla looked at Leo, then over at Shawn and said, "I need some of that."

Shawn responded with his best cat-ate-the-canary grin. Leo handed Carla a napkin.

"No, thank you," she said, "I'm not a fan of caviar."

"I'm sorry," said Leo, "I guess I misunderstood."

Shawn watched Carla watching Leo. "Leo Ventura," he said, "say hello to Carla Montgomery. You, of course, are familiar with the name? Carla, this is Leo Ventura, a hugely talented artist I think you need to know." Shawn took the tray out of Leo's hands. "Why don't I take over the fish egg disbursement while you two get acquainted. I think you'll find it could be mutually beneficial. A win-win, as they say."

Leo hesitated, "But I should be serving."

"Not if I say you should be socializing," said Shawn. "Don't worry, Leo Ventura, I'll square things with Jack. And remember, he who hesitates, loses everything." Then to Carla,"Leo Ventura. Don't you love the sound of that? Leo Ventura. It's like a ride through the hills of Tuscany on a beautiful spring day. Don't you think?"

He winked at Leo. "Don't be frightened Leo. She won't bite...but she might ask you to."

Carla swatted Shawn on the butt. "Be gone, you. Go sparkle someplace else."

Shawn tilted his head in a slight bow, then walked through the party, tray held high, calling,"Fresh eggs! Any takers?"

Carla Montgomery took Leo Ventura home that night. She changed his life forever.

20. Murder in the Abstract

Signing up.

Today's a painting day, all day. I'm working on a large-scale, abstracted landscape. Part of an ongoing series. Compositionally, it plays with space. Conceptually, it plays with altered perception. Aesthetically, it's going for high drama, grand opera. Sounds good anyway. We'll see.

The silence is interrupted, thankfully, by my phone doing the mambo thing.

"Hello."

"Mr. Ryder?" It's a man's voice.

"Yes."

"Mr. Able Ryder, the artist?"

"That would be me."

"Mr. Ryder, this is Detective Jerry Maroney of the New York Police Department. We're investigating the death of Carla Montgomery. I was wondering if I could have a moment of your time."

"Yes, of course detective, but I don't know what I'll be able to tell you. I didn't actually know Miss Montgomery that well."

I hear the sound of papers being shuffled in the background. "Well, I'm looking at a picture that implies otherwise."

"We went out, dated, a couple of times, years and years ago. Since then, we would run into each other socially on occasion; but we weren't close friends. No Christmas cards. No hearts on Instagram."

"I see. Nevertheless, I'd still like to have a few words. Any thoughts from anyone who knew her intimately, would be helpful. I'll be coming down to Pennsylvania tomorrow. I'd like to come by, if that's possible. Otherwise..."

"No, tomorrow will be fine. I do have a guest visiting for the weekend."

"Did they know Ms. Montgomery? Perhaps he or she will have some thoughts as well?"

"Detective, there isn't a topic about which Kate Lindsey has no opinions. And she knew Carla even less than I."

"Ms. Lindsey...yes, Mr. Swann mentioned her as well."

"Hugo? Is that how you got my number?"

"Yes sir. He said you'd be fine with that. He also mentioned that he thought you weren't too far from Bryn Mawr. Is that right?"

"About an hour and twenty minutes away. Not close. Not far. Why do you ask?"

"I've got an appointment to see Ms. Montgomery's family; her mother, her brother... what's his name? I've got it here somewhere."

Again, with the rustling of papers in the background...

"Thorne," I say, "Her brother's name is Thorne. Short for Hawthorne. And her sister's name is Sidney."

"Sidney. That's right. See, Mr. Ryder, you knew her better than you thought."

"Yes, detective, I guess I did. Tell me, will Sidney also be at her parent's tomorrow?"

Sidney is Carla's younger sister, eight years younger. She's an artist, a painter, like me; and well on her way to a successful career, no thanks to any encouragement from her big sister. Ironic, or hypocritical, as it may seem, Carla never supported women in the arts. She said, loudly and clearly, that she believed it was a man's domain. This didn't win her a lot of fans among the female artistic community, but it made for good copy; and Carla knew self-promotion even better than she knew art.

Whether she truly believed that, no one was actually sure; but her public stance had created headlines, and a rift between her and Sidney that evolved over time into a wall of mutual contempt. Sidney was already envious of Carla's glamorous beauty and incisive intellect; now she came to see her as a calculating opportunist; a politician among the intelligentsia. Carla, for her part, had always admired Sidney's inborn creativity and quirky allure; but she found her artistic idealism naive and her actual talent marginal at best. She recommended her sister drop the artist pose and go into a field more suited to her abilities - working at a cosmetics counter perhaps, or photo styling.

War had been declared. A cold war. Sidney pursued her chosen career and avoided any mention of or contact with her famous sister, coincidentally adding to her own mystique as a result. Carla never acknowledged Sidney at all, even as it became fairly unavoidable not to do so. As Sidney's star rose in the east, Carla didn't denigrate her work, nor did she applaud her effort. She simply ignored her.

Personally, I'm a fan of Sidney Chase Montgomery, the artist and the woman. I've met her several times over the years and we know a lot of the same people. She's beautiful in a very different way than her sister – dark brown, very short hair; enormous doe eyes; pale, pale skin; long, long legs; a beautiful tomboy, like Jean Seberg in Breathless. She has wit and style and a personal aesthetic all about color on a large scale; canvases of great beauty, both delicate and forceful in their execution. That's Sidney.

"Yes, Mr. Ryder, she'll be there, too...Mr. Ryder, perhaps you and your guest would accompany me to the Montgomery's? It could make the visit feel less cold. A familiar face, and all..."

"Perhaps," said Able, "Let's see tomorrow."

21. Making Plans

Had I known, I would have packed differently.

It's later that same day and the diva has landed. Over dinner, I tell Kate about the phone call from Detective Maroney and his request for help.

"I told him I'd think about it. It could be interesting."

"Or deadly dull. Oops, I guess that's not an appropriate word to be using. So, when is this Hardy Boys adventure supposed to begin?"

"Actually, Nancy Drew, he's meeting us here tomorrow morning."

"You roped me into this, too?"

"As if you wouldn't be interested. Besides which, you need a change. We both know that."

"You know, I always have loved mysteries."

"I know. And you always have hated Carla Montgomery. Admit it, you're dying to know what happened."

"Again with the 'dying'. Don't say 'dying' to a murder investigator."

"Then you'll do it?"

"Well, I *am* curious. It was all over the papers for a few days, then disappeared. Have you heard anything?"

"Hugo says her family used their connections to hold off the press; that's why you haven't read any more about it. He also says her most recent boyfriend, a young artist named Leo Ventura, is the prime suspect. Apparently Leo cuts his canvases with a knife when he's done painting."

"Oh you madcap artists, you."

"I guess we'll learn more when the detective arrives tomorrow."

"Not too early I hope. I'd like to sleep for possibly ever..."

"Kate? You're drifting. Still here?"

"I was just wondering...should I wear a hat? I always think female detectives should wear hats. They add an air of mystery and yet they're so professional. What do you think?"

"I think the martinis have kicked in. And I think it's time for bed."

22. What Was the Question?

Who has the answer?

The detective arrives around 1:00. He's a serious, thirty-something guy, not unpleasant, just very proper. Official. Removed. He wears a clearly un-tailored grey suit, white shirt, rep stripe tie, spit-polished shoes. He looks like a supporting actor, a second lead – handsome, but not too handsome; tall, but not too tall; average in a studied way. Kate agrees with me but thinks it gives him a Clark Kent appeal – grey suit not withstanding, it's pretty obvious the man has muscle. Kate is clearly pleased. She loves a challenge.

I offer the detective a cup of coffee, and we all sit down to discuss the investigation of Carla Montgomery's murder. We start with a series of routine questions to verify that we have alibis for the evening in question. Our alibis, of course, are each other and everybody else at the Audubon event.

"Isn't this exciting?" says Kate, "I've never been accused of murder before. Are you going to frisk me, too, Detective Maroney?"

The detective doesn't smile. "No, ma'am, that won't be necessary."

"You'll have to excuse Miss Lindsey, she's a little confused about her role in today's proceedings, aren't you dearest?"

"I was only trying to be thorough."

I read her expression to say, 'Oh, Able, let me enjoy myself. He's cute.'

She reads mine to reply, 'He's not that cute, and he's young enough to be your little brother.'

'Killjoy.'

'Chickenhawk.'

The detective interrupts our closed-caption conversation with a well-placed clearing of his throat. "Ahem. If we could continue."

"I'm sorry, Detective Maroney. We must have wandered off," says Kate.

"Yes. We do that some times," I add. "Sorry, it won't happen again."

The questioning continues in various directions alluding to our interactions with that level of society, our opinions of Carla Montgomery – her public persona and private one, the art world in general, our thoughts of a long list of names – some we each knew personally, some we'd only read about on *Gawker* or *People* online.

When he seems satisfied, he tells us what's known for certain about that night:

Carla had called for car service to drive her to Bucks County, Pennsylvania. She was expected at an event for the Audubon Society later that evening.Thomas, the night doorman in Carla's building, buzzed her intercom at around 4:30 to let her know the car had arrived.

Five minutes later, Carla's body was discovered by her next-door neighbor, Mrs. Joan Leighton, a widow in her early seventies who lives alone with her toy collie named Chappy. Mrs. Leighton had been out walking her dog. She returned to find Carla slumped over in her open doorway and to see someone stepping into the other elevator. She couldn't tell if it was a man or a woman. The figure was "medium height, medium build", dressed all in black with a large black trench coat, collar turned up, and a black baseball cap pulled low over his or her face.

Mrs. Leighton rushed into her own apartment and locked the door, then immediately called Tommy, who called the police. They arrived momentarily. The police found no sign of struggle, no sign of forced entry, no fingerprints and no evidence of robbery. Carla had been stabbed twice from the front and her throat had been slashed with a 6" or 7" blade by someone who had a strong, sure stroke.

The detective had arrived at the scene shortly after the police. He conducted a search of the apartment and found everything intact. He retained her iPhone, which was lying on the floor with the evening bag and keys, and her journal, which was sitting on one of the night tables by the bed, for evidence and information.

"... and that brings me to you, Mr. Ryder and Ms. Lindsey."

Kate is the first to respond. "It's Able and Kate, Detective Jerry, and I think your presentation was wonderful. Well done!"

I roll my eyes. "So, how is it you came to speak with Hugo Swann?"

"Ms. Montgomery had an entry in her phone," he reaches in his very worn brief case and pulls out a log of Carla's phone contents. As he leafs through the texts, e mails and calendar postings, he continues, "Mr. Swann's name pops up a lot, but most importantly, it's the first name to show up after Friday, the day she was killed. It was a reminder to see new work at Mr. Swann's gallery...here it is, NEW SHOW AT HUGO SWANN. SPEAK WITH H.S. RE: L.V. Mr. Swann says Ms. Montgomery dropped in regularly to see what was new and to talk shop; find out what people are buying. We're guessing L.V. stands for Leo Ventura."

"The knife artist," I say

"D'you know him?"

"At this point, everyone who reads the news knows him. But, no, personally we've never met."

"Mr. Swann says that Ms. Montgomery would occasionally promote new talent to him... try to hook them up. He said she also acted as a freelance dealer, so, if he wasn't interested in her artists, maybe he knew somebody who would be."

"Well, I don't imagine Hugo would be very interested in Ventura's work, from what I've heard about it. Hugo shows more representational painting, whereas Ventura's sounds more..."

"Cutting edge?" Kate interjects. "Sorry. I couldn't resist."

Detective Maroney does not look up from his note pad.

"But seriously," says Kate, looking sideways at me, "No, I mean it. You don't really think Leo Ventura had anything to do with the murder do you? She was killed with a knife, he works with a knife. It's too obvious, don't you think? Maybe someone else used a knife so you'd assume it was him."

"Do you watch a lot of TV, Kate?" asks the detective.

I choke on my coffee, "She's in advertising, Jerry. It's part of her job."

Kate shoots me a withering look, aka *Kate Face*, "Thanks for coming to my defense."

"I'm sorry, " says the detective, "It's just that in TV, you'd be absolutely right; but in the real world, the obvious guy usually did it. We don't dismiss them right off the bat."

"So you do think Leo Ventura did it?" she asks.

"It's not that easy. I wouldn't be asking these questions if it was. Apparently Ms. Montgomery made a lot of enemies over the years..."

Kate nudges me, "See. I was right about that."

The detective continues, "...and there are a lot of unclear notes and entries in her phone calendar and journal. It seems that she was involved with several men at the same time..."

"No!" says Kate. "Well I, for one, am shocked."

"...and it doesn't look like she had many women friends, you know, like a best girl friend who knew her better than anyone?"

"Oh," I interrupt. "You mean Shawn Patrik. Shawn was Carla's best friend."

"His name came up often. I assumed he was one of the men she was seeing."

"Shawn doesn't go out with women."

"Oh?" he thinks for a second.

As we continue to discuss Carla's life and the players involved, Kate and I give the wide-eyed detective a crash course in the goings on of high society and the culture club – who's friends with whom, who's sleeping with what, who owes whom a favor, and what's the pecking order. I fill him in on Carla's role as high priestess of the arts, while Kate gives him the background, albeit with a fair amount of editorializing, on Carla Montgomery, the femme fatale.

An hour goes by when the detective looks at his watch, closes his note pad and stands up, getting ready to go. "Thank you both for your time and input. It's been very helpful, I assure you. You each have a unique relationship to this social world. Should anything come to mind that you think would benefit us in our investigation, please don't hesitate to call."

He hands each of us his business card. "And now, I should be off to my next appointment. Mr. Ryder, Ms. Lindsey, would you care to accompany me to the Chase Montgomery's? These aren't normal circumstances. I know that Mr. Ryder knows these people and you, Ms. Lindsey, I'm guessing, are comfortable in any situation. Considering the interaction we've already had during this investigation with members of the privileged class, we're in favor of anything we can do to make our interrogations seem less adversarial and more..."

"Social?" I ask.

"Precisely."

"Able, I feel a career change coming on," Kate says, smiling in my direction. She looks at Detective Maroney and notices a slight twitch at the corner of his mouth.

"Why detective, is that a smile I see? Yes, I think it is. Able, Detective Jerry's smiling. I think he likes us."

23. M is for the Million Things She Gave Us

Love you. Mean it.

Sidney Montgomery is drying off, fresh from a late morning shower, when she looks up and sees her brother, Thorne, standing in the doorway.

"Jesus! You scared me! How long have you been standing there?"

"Long enough. I always said you were the pretty one. I was right."

"Well, you look like hell. Late night?" She wraps the towel around her, sarong style, and turns to face the mirror.

"I don't know. Is 9:00 a.m. a late night?" Thorne comes up behind her and puts his arms around her waist. "Ummm, you smell good."

Sidney pulls his arms away. "And you just smell. Get away from me, or I'll have to take another shower."

"What a lousy thing to say to your only living sibling." He sits down on the edge of the tub and lights a cigarette. "Isn't tragedy supposed to bring us closer together?"

"I'd kill for a cigarette, if that's what you mean," she reaches forward, takes Thorne's out of his mouth, and places it in her own, as she proceeds to comb her hair. "Are you going to change for our guests, or are you staying like that, in costume – the dissipated trust fund baby?"

"Would you prefer it if I went all Ralph Lauren-y and appeared at the terrace doors, racquet in hand, calling, 'Tennis anyone?'"

"Well, Mother would love it."

"Mother wouldn't notice, one way or the other. Mother is arranging roses and setting tea, as if her garden club is coming, not some low-life investigator who's hoping to find out just how we all felt about our brilliant and beautiful and very dead sister. No, Sid, mother is completely dazed."

"It's called mourning, Thorne."

"It's called Lexapro, Sid, washed down with a little vodka and orange juice, only hold that orange juice...it's so fattening, all that pulp!"

Sidney watches her brother in the mirror...her handsome, baby brother. So tall. So fine. So pathetic. 'I take after my mother,' he was fond of saying. And he did, God help him. Their mother is a beautiful woman. Chic, elegant, poised...and a serious drunk with a tiny little prescription drug problem. Strangers say she has an ethereal presence. Friends call her delicate and wistful. Her children know otherwise.

Cassandra Chase Montgomery is that rarest of rare jewels – a direct line Mayflower descendant on both her mother's and father's sides. She's the real thing, a WASP dream; Old Philadelphia money and a natural blonde, at least once upon a time.

Cassandra and her slightly younger sister, Penelope, were on the cover of LIFE magazine before they reached their twentieth birthdays. The accompanying article described lives of immeasurable privilege; and the photos portrayed a level of confidence and ease that can only be attained through great beauty, greater wealth and never having been said 'no' to.

Hard to believe that just one year after that article, Penelope would be found dead of an accidental overdose of sleeping pills, and Cassandra would find herself trapped in a horribly unhappy, but socially very appropriate, marriage. A marriage arranged by her parents to offset the negative publicity of Penelope's unfortunate incident, as well as to connect the Chase name to another honorable, albeit insolvent, Philadelphia family; the Montgomerys.

Cassandra Chase first met Charles Montgomery through her sister. Penelope and Charles had had a summer romance in Capri, where both were visiting the families of boarding school friends. Cassandra, Penelope, and, it seemed, Charles had all been studying in Switzerland that year. Cassandra, always more serious than her fun-loving sister, was spending that summer in Paris where she had enrolled in the art history program being offered at the Louvre. She came down one week in July for a little sun and sand; it was then that she met this big bear of a guy, all shoulders and ego, who had rescued Penelope, or so she put it, from her virginity. There was nothing Cassandra could find in him to like. Penelope, though, seemed entranced.

Cassandra cut her week long holiday short and headed back to the comforts of Monet and Cezanne. She had found herself in the study of art, and her short break in Capri had made her realize just how much it had come to mean to her. Cassandra and Penelope, always so close growing up, were becoming more and more different from each other. Penelope was all laughter and sparkle, taking big bites out of life and inviting everyone to join her. Cassandra, though more truly beautiful, had always been the quieter of the two; and even while she displayed an outer shell of grace and nonchalance, she always felt a little out of place – and time.

When she discovered art, she discovered the language she was meant to speak, and the sensitivity and beauty she longed for. By the end of that summer, Cassandra was filled with hope for a new kind of future. Her life would be different from her mother's and her sister's and the lives of her friends. Not just society, not just formality, but a life filled with creativity and ideas.

At the end of summer, when she returned home to Bryn Mawr, her parents told her that Penelope had decided to stay on in Europe through the fall term. She thought nothing of it, at first, assuming that life had gotten as busy for Penelope as it had for her. She was also guessing that Charles Montgomery was still in the picture but didn't want to bring this to her parents' attention. Why alarm them? And why get Penelope in trouble for what Cassandra hoped would be a short-lived fling?

Penelope didn't come home until the spring. Cassandra missed her sister and was so looking forward to catching up with her. However, when she saw Penelope, she was shocked. The dazzle was gone. The spark, missing. She looked fragile and afraid. When Cassandra tried to speak to her, she smiled sadly, and just looked away. Their mother explained that Penelope had lost a close friend in a tragic accident the previous month, and it had shaken her quite a bit, but it was nothing to be alarmed at. They had already met with the family doctor who said all she needed was a good rest.

Two months later, after not much change, Penelope took an overdose of sleeping pills and said goodbye to life. When Cassandra discovered her in her bedroom, she was holding a note which read, 'I'm sorry. I can't.' Nothing more.

Sorry about what? Can't what? Cassandra didn't understand. Was this really happening? Would she never hear her sister's vibrant laughter, or see her glorious smile ever again? And who was this tragic friend, a friend who's death had sent Penelope into a fatal tail spin? A friend she had never mentioned to Cassandra. Had they grown that far apart? It was a mystery. It didn't make sense. Nothing made sense. Her own overwhelming grief was only made survivable by the bizarre feeling that none of this was real.

Her parents certainly behaved as if everything was fine and perfectly normal. One never would have guessed that they had lost their cherished young daughter to suicide. Of course, to them it was a horrible accident. An unfortunate mistake. Penelope had been confused. She certainly never meant to do such a thing. A statement was given to the press saying Penelope had died from an infection she had contracted in France. Mrs. Chase explained to Cassandra that any public display of grief was considered unseemly and inappropriate. Any mourning should only be carried out in private. Alone. 'And no make up or jewelry at the funeral, darling,' Mrs. Chase would say, 'that would be vulgar.'

So, when her mother said, on the night of Penelope's funeral, that the family needed a wedding – a happy event to wash away this unpleasantness – Cassandra pulled herself deeper into the empty space where her heart had been. She didn't know her mother anymore, this perfect, soulless ice sculpture of a woman. And she had never really known her father, that man at the end of the dinner table, who smelled of expensive cigars, and had always looked at both Cassandra and her sister as if they were possessions – no better or worse than the carpet beneath his feet or the chandelier which hung over his head.

No mother. No father. No sister. Cassandra's life was disappearing. She was disappearing. And now. her mother would have her marry...someone. "Of course, Mother. Whatever you think best, Mother. Certainly Mother." She thought she should cry, but there were no tears. She thought she should scream, but no one would hear her. So, in the end, she said yes.

The fact that the groom her parents had chosen for her turned out to be Charles Montgomery – the same Charles Montgomery who had deflowered her sister and somehow, Cassandra knew, contributed to her death; a man Cassandra had disliked on sight – somehow seemed fitting. A perfectly hollow man for a perfectly hollow marriage. She would have laughed, but there was no joy. Only a growing emptiness.

Her mother arranged everything, of course; and Cassandra was the perfect bride, of course. The hundreds of guests were suitably impressed and comforted by this very public affirmation of the charmed way of life they all shared. "We were so sorry to hear about Penelope," they seemed to say, "but isn't the reception wonderful? And don't you love the canapes?'"

The groom was of little importance or interest, to Cassandra or the wedding guests. What mattered was that he was 'Our kind'. A familiar name, a pleasant mother, no great fortune to speak of, but ancestors who mattered. Money wasn't an issue, anyway. Cassandra was the one with the money. Everyone knew that. Now her husband, Mr., what-was-his-name-again? Oh yes, Mr. Charles Montgomery. Well, he would now have a promising career as Mr. Cassandra Chase.

Once again the status quo had been maintained.

On their wedding night, a very drunk Charles attempted to seduce his beautiful bride. When she feigned a headache, Charles struck her. She didn't cry. She didn't really care. Charles, becoming more and more ugly, taunted his new wife, comparing her to Penelope, saying Penelope was a great lay, that she'd do anything, and that they used to make fun of proper, frigid Cassandra. Still, Cassandra didn't respond. He called her useless, he called her stupid. He didn't stop. Nothing affected her. Nothing. Until he brought up the baby.

He hadn't meant to. The words flew out of his mouth before he could stop them. He wasn't supposed to mention it. Ever. That was part of the deal, the arrangement he had made with Mr. and Mrs. Chase. Cassandra was never to know.

She came at him, pounding his chest, clawing at his face, "What did you do to Penelope?! What did you do?!"

Suddenly sober, Charles grabbed her wrists and held Cassandra away from him Cassandra took a deep breath and coldly collected herself.

"Tell – me – everything," she said in quiet measured tones.

Charles let her go and stepped over to the chaise, where he sat down, pressing his temples with his fingertips. Cassandra stayed where she was, standing next to the bed, never taking her eyes off of him.

He began to speak in a small, sad voice. He told her about Penelope, about meeting her for the first time on the beach. He told her how they'd fallen in love; and when Cassandra looked into his eyes, she believed him. He said they loved each other's wild side, their adventurous natures, in sex and everything else. He had been her first. They spoke of marriage, but Penelope told him she didn't want to get married, she was too young. She wanted this to be a special summer romance for both of them; and if, in the future, they came together again, that would be their fate. But no marriage, not just yet.

Then, they found out Penelope was pregnant. They'd always been careful; but somehow, something must have gone wrong. He wanted her to have an abortion. He'd pay for it. She said no, she wanted to have the baby. They had a huge fight, but made up quickly, with Charles coming around to her side; but, he insisted, they were definitely getting married. She said yes.

Charles stood up and walked over to the terrace doors, looking out at - what? The past, perhaps. He continued with his tale.

"Very early on in the pregnancy, Penelope had complications. We were scared. We had no choice but to tell your parents, hoping they'd get over their initial shock and then help us get the proper care for Pen and the baby. Your mother was amazing, making all the necessary arrangements and promising to keep things quiet. She came to see us several times in the last year," Charles looked over at Cassandra's baffled expression, "You didn't know, of course. Probably thought she was visiting relatives or shopping in New York. She took care of everything and never scolded, never reproached us." Charles grinned ironically and added, "Your mother would've made a great politician." His grin vanished and his face became blank with grief, "We didn't know what we would have done without her."

"Penelope got through the worst of it, months really, and counted the days to her delivery. Your mother convinced her that the logical thing to do, for everyone's sake, was to have the baby, leave it in the care of a foster family she had found, then come home to America, announce the engagement and, in an appropriate period of time, get married. After our honeymoon, we would announce the news that Penelope was pregnant. We would go to a clinic in Switzerland for the final months of her pregnancy, presumably, but in fact, would be going to Paris to pick up our baby from the foster family. We would come home as one big happy family, and no one would be the wiser.

Charles paused in his story. He stared at the floor. Cassandra broke the silence.

"What happened, Charles?"

"It was a Sunday morning last April. Pen was staying with friends of your parents', the

Chesters, in Paris. Your mother was also there that weekend for a visit. I was living in a boarding house they had found for me. I went to the Chesters, as I did every day for breakfast. There was a flower vendor on the way where I'd stop and buy your sister small bunches of violets. She loved violets..." His voice cracked; he continued.

"When I arrived, Claudine, the maid, told me Pen had been rushed to the hospital not an hour before. She'd spiked a fever overnight and had started bleeding. Something was wrong with the baby. I hurried across town to the hospital and was met in the waiting room by your mother, looking poised and perfect as always. I was crazed, frantic. She took my arm and motioned me toward one of the waiting room benches. She spoke in a calm, controlled voice, saying that Penelope was going to be fine, but the baby was gone.

"I was numb, confused. Elated that Pen was all right. Shattered that the baby had died. I didn't know what to do next. But your mother, once again, had thought of everything. She said she thought it would be best if I didn't see Pen for a while, she had arranged for my return flight to Philadelphia. I was leaving that afternoon. She would stay on in Paris and handle any messy details as she put it.

"'Get on with your life', she said, 'there's no reason this unfortunate incident need affect your future.' The implication was clear; the Chase family was done with me. There would be no wedding. There would be no future."

Cassandra was overwhelmed by what she was hearing. Where had she been all those months? Studying, socializing, enjoying her life, while half way around the world, her sister was scared and suffering. And all the while, her mother was keeping the truth from her. From everyone.

Charles continued. "They kept us apart after that. I wrote to her, but the letters came back unopened. I phoned the Chesters, but they wouldn't take my calls. I contacted the hospital, but they wouldn't release any information. A month later, I found out that your mother and Pen had come back to Philadelphia right after I had. They'd been here all along. I tried to see her, but your parents wouldn't allow it. Your father offered me a check for $25,000 if I would just disappear from your family's life. I was angry, frustrated...helpless.

"Then...you know Abby Daniels? Of course you do. Abby had been to visit Penelope."

"I remember," interrupted Cassandra, "It was the week before Penelope died."

"Yes," Charles was pacing back and forth in the middle of the room. "Abby had been our confidante in Capri. She knew everything. Pen gave Abby a letter to deliver to me." He stopped and turned toward the closet. He took out his suitcase, opened it and reached into the side compartment, pulling out a pale blue envelope which he handed to Cassandra. She let out a low sigh as she recognized her sister's handwriting.

"Read it. Please." he said.

Cassandra took the letter from the envelope and began.

'Dear Charles,

They won't let me see you. I'm lost and so alone. Cassandra tries to cheer me up, but she doesn't know our story. Mother says it's best this way. I don't know, maybe she's right.

We're young still. And time heals everything, right?

All I know is I love you and miss you and I want to see you. I want to tell Cassandra everything. I love her, too. Just you and Cassandra. She and I have never kept the truth from each other. But mother says 'no', she's too delicate to deal with our sordid little tale...I don't know...maybe it's the medicine...I'm so confused. And empty. So empty.

Mother said adoption was the right thing to do. But I miss the baby. Our baby. I can't go on, not like this.

Know that I love you. And know that I'm sorry. We'll be together again, some day.

- your Pen

Cassandra looked up from the letter and stared ahead into nothing. A baby, she thought. Somewhere there was a baby. Her gaze shifted to Charles. He was watching her with an expression she couldn't read.

"Charles, what did you do when you received the letter?"

"I...I didn't know about the baby. You have to believe me."

"I do."

"I sent a message to your mother saying that I knew everything and we had to talk. She responded to that message and agreed to see me. But the day before we were to meet, Penelope...had killed herself. And do you know how I found out? Your father had his lawyer come to my house with a blank check and a contract stating, now that Penelope was dead, I would never tell what had happened between us. I would never mention or seek out the baby, and I would never cross paths with your family again. If I agreed to sign, he would give me a check for $1,000,000.

"I was in a rage! I told the lawyer it would take a lot more than that to keep me quiet. That I would drag your family's name through the mud and I wouldn't stop until I had everything. Your father's response was that you were to inherit everything and he wouldn't turn you out. However, if I agreed to marry you, then I would benefit from your inheritance, and he would benefit, in so much as I wouldn't want to destroy the reputation of my own family."

Cassandra saw everything very clearly now. "So, in honor of my sister's memory, you blackmailed my father?"

Charles said nothing.

"You know, of course, that the negotiations were all Mother's doing. Father just writes the checks. He controls the money, but she controls the melodrama." Cassandra folded her sister's letter and tucked it inside the bodice of her gown. She slowly stood up and walked to the terrace doors.

"So... I've been sold. One sister's future for another sister's past."

"Cassandra, I never meant to hurt you. It was never about you. It was about revenge. For Penelope's sake."

"For Penelope?" her voice rose. "You have a child, Charles. Or did you forget that? This had nothing to do with Penelope or the baby or me. It was all about the money. Money and appearances. You wanted to be rich. Well, now you are. You wanted to marry a Chase and so you have," Cassandra's tone changed from anger to disdain, "and to think that I believed you really cared for her. You can be very convincing – to a point. Poor Charles. Poor, pathetic Charles."

"What are you going to do, Cassandra?"

"Do? Oh, so many things. I do intend to honor my parents' contract with you. We're married. And will stay that way. And you will say nothing about my sister's pregnancy or child or death – ever. However Charles, what you don't understand is that, in many ways, I am my father's daughter. I will control your allowance and all expenditures. Your wealth is totally tied to me. Should anything happen to me, I will make sure that you get nothing.

"Then, why not buy me out of the marriage?"

"It's too expensive. And I don't trust you. Besides, I think you can be useful. I don't much care for men, never have. But I would like children, and I think you would make attractive, healthy children. I would like two, I think. Once that has been accomplished, you can do whatever you like with whomever you chose. I just ask that you be discreet."

"And what if I want out?"

"You'll get out when I say so."

Charles looked confused by the woman before him. This was not the meek Cassandra he had assumed her to be.

"One more thing, Charles, and this is very important. We are finding Penelope's baby and we are bringing that baby home."

24. There's No Place Like Home

It's the third estate on the left.

"You know, I've always thought Bryn Mawr made Beverly Hills look like Levittown," Kate's enjoying the view from the back seat of Detective Maroney's grey Ford, "This is *real* money."

"Actually," I say, "Gladwynne's the real money. A lot of Bryn Mawr is illusion."

"Then a grand illusion it is!"

"You mean, that castle over there isn't real?" asks the detective.

"No, it's real; but it's probably half empty. This is an old money town. And a lot of the old money has been split up among too many kids and grandkids. Many of these houses, as beautiful as they are, are too expensive to maintain and too big to sell. That one over there was turned into condos a long time ago, and the brick monster up ahead on the right has been vacant for at least twenty years."

"How is it you know so much, Able?" asks the detective.

"Able grew up around all of this," Kate replies, grandly sweeping her arm from side to side.

"Really?"

"Not quite. I grew up nearby. On the other side of the tracks. Near the bubble gum factory."

"Spare me the *Mildred Pierce* narration," sighs Kate, "It may not have been Main Line, but it was no Tobacco Road, either. Able grew up in a pretty, little town twenty minutes that way," she points out the back window."

"There *was* a bubble gum factory, and it *is* on the other side of the tracks," I respond "Anyway, I did grow up nearby and I knew some of these families from high school and college."

"Did you know the Chases or Montgomerys back then?" asks the detective.

"No, but I knew of them. Now, *they're* the real thing. Mrs. Montgomery', as you know, is a Chase, and she inherited her family's entire fortune, which she tripled over the years. She's a very shrewd business woman, and every inch the lady of the manor. Cassandra Chase Montgomery is classic, old style Philadelphia, like Grace Kelly."

"Love that," Kate interjects,"Cashmere sweater sets and pearls – lots and lots of pearls. And perfect posture. And always the right thing to say. And maybe, just maybe, a little too much gin before 5:00."

"Got the picture," says the detective. "How about Mr. Montgomery?"

"He married the money and never worked a day in his life. He's got everything a man could want – except love, respect, purpose......and here we are. Make the next right, detective."

We drive through the open gate and up the winding driveway, eventually reaching the main house, a beautiful white Federalist-style structure, not unlike a certain white house in Washington, D.C. – perhaps a little larger. A servant appears at the front door to welcome us. Detective Maroney helps Kate out of the car.

"Well, that's impressive," he says.

"Did you say impressive or oppressive?" she responds.

I step ahead of them and introduce myself and Kate and Jerry to the butler, who replies,"Mrs. Chase Montgomery is expecting you. If you would be so good as to follow me..."

He leads the way through a spacious, beautifully appointed Jefferson-era entrance foyer with early family portraits by Raeburn and Peale; past the formal living room with it's elegant, late 19th century French furnishings and enormous Sargent portrait of Mrs. Chase Montgomery's grandmother. We're greeted at the entry to the garden room by Mrs. Chase Montgomery, herself, dressed in pale beige Valentino cashmere and her afternoon pearls.

Perfect.

25. Thanks for Stopping By

Don't be a stranger.

She offers both of her hands to me and says,"Able. The detective told me you would be joining us when he phoned this morning. It was good of you to come."

"And you must be Miss Lindsey. How do you do? I am Cassandra Chase Montgomery." She graciously shakes hands with Kate, who can not take her eyes off of the still very beautiful woman.

"Mrs. Chase Montgomery," the detective steps forward, "I'm Detective Maroney."

She takes his hand and holds it tightly. "Thank you for coming all this way to see us and for trying to find out who did this terrible thing to our lovely..." her trembling voice fades completely. She looks delicate...breakable...like a porcelain figurine.

"We'll do everything we can, ma'am."

"Cassandra," I say softly, "why don't we all sit down over here. I see you've set tea for us. How kind." I look to Kate for verbal assistance.

"Mrs. Chase Montgomery, your home is beautiful. Oh, and look at the gardens! How wonderful!" Kate steps over to the window, "So many roses. Oh, I do love roses – receiving them more than growing them, I must confess."

Cassandra smiles sweetly.

Kate goes on, "I've never been very good in the garden, I'm afraid. All thumbs and none of them green." She removes her hat and sits down across from Cassandra, "Fortunately I have other talents, or so I'm told."

"I think I've just witnessed one of them," says Cassandra. "Thank you for being here, Miss Lindsey."

"Shall I pour?" Kate asks.

"Yes, please."

"The children should be here momentarily, and their father – well, I expect him home soon. Ah, here they are now. Sidney, Thorne, come say hello to our guests. Sidney, you know Able Ryder, of course."

"Hello, Able. I'd say 'good to see you' but somehow that doesn't seem appropriate."

There is no attempt made at solemnity or respect for the occasion.

"I was so sorry to hear about Carla."

"Sorry? I doubt that. Surprised maybe. Then again, maybe not." Sidney looks over at Detective Maroney. "You must be the investigator."

"Yes, Miss. Detective Jerry Maroney, Miss. How do you do?"

"Fine thanks. And you?'

Clearly he doesn't like her tone. "Fine. Thank you."

"And I'm Kate Lindsey, Miss Chase Montgomery. I'm a great admirer of your work."

"Hello Ms. Lindsey. Thank you," she responds with a complete lack of interest in whom Kate is and what she's just said. Kate is not amused, but smiles kindly, just the same.

Sidney continues, "Everyone, this is my little brother, Thorne. Thorne, say hello to the nice people."

Thorne throws himself into the nearest chair and grabs for the tray of tea sandwiches.

"You'll have to excuse my brother," says Sidney, "he has a birth defect. He's rude."

Cassandra stares at her daughter with contempt and the temperature of the room grows suddenly cold. Then she smiles a motherly smile and comes to her son's defense, "He doesn't mean to be, do you dear heart? He's just been working so hard lately and not sleeping very well, isn't that right, Thorne?" Her voice is calm. Her face is insistent.

"Yes, mother. Whatever you say, mother."

"Detective," says Cassandra, "Perhaps we should begin the interview. Let's not wait for Charles. He may have been detained."

"Oh yes," blurts out Thorne, "Let's not wait for daddy. We could be waiting for a long, long time!" he starts to laugh.

"Shut up, Thorne," says Sidney.

"That's enough, Thorne," says Cassandra sternly.

"Who knows where he could be or with whom?"

"I said that's enough!" Both of her children are visibly fearful of their mother's sudden vitriol. Cassandra composes herself. "As you can see, my son…all of us…we're all very distressed by our…by Carla's death." She takes a deep breath and lowers her eyelids for just one second. "Now then, may we proceed?"

Sidney and Thorne relax back into their arrogant posturing – it just isn't quite as convincing as before. One big happy family, I think to myself, and as I look toward Kate, I realize she's having the identical thought.

26. Q&A

I beg your pardon?

Questioning goes on for an hour. Thorne never eases up on his complete disdain for the detective, so Kate and I smooth the way whenever we can. He's obviously more interested in the tea sandwiches than he is in his murdered older sister. Admittedly, he admired Carla, was somewhat in awe of her, always felt she was daddy's favorite. They'd never been close – too much of an age difference – and once she'd moved to New York, he saw her mostly in the news, like everyone else. That's how he found out she'd died. It didn't really mean too much to him. He was sorry and all that, but, you know, whatever.

Sidney, on the other hand, is remarkably candid about her feelings for Carla - she hated her. And unlike her brother, she isn't sorry she's gone. To Sidney, Carla was a user. A self-absorbed, self-serving manipulator who deserved whatever she got. Sidney was at a party on the night in question – an easy alibi to verify. Did she know who may have done it? "No," she said, "but I'd love to find out, so I could send them a thank-you note."

As the hour wears on, the source of Cassandra Chase Montgomery's calm becomes more evident. Her head bobs ever so slightly, her eyelids lower now and then, just the least bit. The muscles around her mouth twitch beneath the surface of her perfect skin. She doesn't drink tea with the rest of them. Instead, her maid brings her her own special brew which she seems to enjoy.

Cassandra tells us of how she had introduced all of her children to the world of art.

"Sidney, of course, had a gift; an inborn talent. She's an artist. Has been since birth. Thorne had no interest, or so he says, but I know he is destined for greatness. Such sensitivity. Such beautiful hands...

"And then there was Carla. Not an artist, per se, but a work of art, do you know? Life was her canvas. People were her medium." Cassandra speaks lovingly about her oldest daughter – her accomplishments, her beauty, her joie de vivre. "Carla lived the life I had once envisioned for myself – a champion of culture surrounded by artistic leaders and creative giants......" She goes on.

Sidney and Thorne pay no attention. They've heard this story many times before.

The detective already knew that Cassandra had been home the night of Carla's murder. He had called her, himself, that same night. Charles was "away on business." Apparently Charles was always "away on business." He still hadn't returned from wherever he had gone that morning, but the detective thinks it would be best to come back and question him another time. The detective thanks the family for their time and promises he will do everything he can to solve Carla's murder. Cassandra is very grateful. Sidney and Thorne couldn't care less.

Once we're all back on the road, Kate is the first to speak, naturally. "The super rich are different from the rest of us. They're totally screwed up. I bet Christmas is a real happy time in the Chase Montgomery household. No wonder Carla was such a shrew with a mother like that."

"But I thought you liked her mother?" I ask, "She liked you."

"Oh please! That's professional charm. Seamless. Highly polished. Doesn't mean squat. Add to that the endless river of boilermakers in her ladyship's tea cup and Cassandra is a dangerous old broad. Beautiful, elegant, and fabulous shoes, but cut you off at the knees, cold-as-steel dangerous. And I think we got a little inside view of *that* Cassandra, didn't we?"

"Don't hold back, tell us how you really feel."

"It's very epic, don't you think? Very Shakespeare. The money, the power, the untold truths. Miss Scarlet in the study with a knife!"

"That was CLUE."

"And what do you think CLUE is, Mr. Smarty? It's Shakespeare – the board game."

"You know, you might have something there. Never underestimate our Ms. Lindsey, Detective Maroney."

Kate's reapplying her lipstick,"Thank you."

"Is anybody hungry?" the detective asks. "The little sandwiches didn't really do it for me."

"I could go for a little something. How about you, Kate?"

"Let's see, what do I feel like? We're in Bryn Mawr...I know! A gimlet!"

"Brilliant!"

"Thought you'd like it."

The detective audibly sighs.

27. I'll Drink to That

Chard and a Pinot Grigio, please.

It's later that same evening. The detective, now lovingly called Detective Jerry or DJ, has gone off to do whatever it is he does. Kate and I have decided to go to our favorite Bucks watering hole (a phrase I particularly enjoy, though it would be more correct to refer to it as our favorite wining hole or, perhaps, whining hole, depending on how the week has progressed). Anyway, it's the *Golden Pheasant* – kindawonderful, delightful staff, delectable dishes, delicious cocktails and beautiful atmosphere with very flattering lighting – always key.

Some people might find it disconcerting when their cocktail order is being poured the moment they arrive, prior to actual ordering. Kate and I see this as a plus, a time-saver and a thoughtful gesture.

Hugs all around. Quick updates with everyone. Love. Love. Kiss. Kiss. It's like a home away from home, where everybody knows your name...but I digress.

We find our seats at the bar and proceed to review the day.

"I'd like to propose a toast," I say. "Here's to real family, whether you're related to them or not."

"Cheers to that!" says Kate. "How weird was today?"

"It's that old annoying thing about people with everything, who don't know how to enjoy it. It's not the money...it's the stuff!"

"Once again, they didn't call us. We could have told them how to enjoy it, stay out of each other's way and just relax! But no, they didn't call."

"They never do."

"Irritating."

"Seriously."

"Some house, though, right?"

"Calling it a house just seems wrong."

"Embassy?"

"How about 'Principality'?"

"I like it. The Principality of Chase Montgomery. Has a ring to it. Like Monaco! Whatever it may be, it's seriously messed up."

"Borderline scary."

"You know, you look around here at the *Pheasant* and you see all of these people and you think, at least I do, *I wonder what we have in common? I wonder where they live? I wonder if they're happy...or not, or contented...or not or busy...or not?* And then I think, *That's what's wonderful about this place, where you just feel a kind of all-inclusive comfort level and people are just glad to see you and they hope you're doing well.* And then I think, *The Chase Montgomerys would never experience something like this, because they would have already sequestered themselves away into a private room, physical or emotional, and they would miss out on that random question like,'So, where are you from?' or 'Do you live around here?' or 'Haven't I seen you at Carroll's Seafood?' or 'Are you gonna eat all of that?'*"

As if on cue, Kimmy, the lovely, young bartender, leans over the bar with refills and says, "It's Kate, isn't it? I remember you coming in with Able about a month ago. Nice to see you."

"Am I melting right now?" says Kate."Point made. That's the best moment of my week, right there."

"Cheers to that! Big money and big fame must be hard, though. But I sure would like to try."

"We can pretend. Why don't we have a *We're Famous Day* tomorrow? Sleep in, get massages, do a little shopping, then reconvene later here for cocktails, onto Chez Ryder for one of your *I-only-have-lettuce-leaves-Tabasco-sauce-and-an-olive-but-here's-your-five-star-meal* meals. Sounds like heaven!"

"Sounds like every weekend. Oh my god, does that mean we're famous? Or rich?!"

"Oh...My...God...I think you're right, Able! We must have forgotten."

28. Rules of the Game

Your move.

Every year Nan and Walter Gibson host The Summer Solstice Gala *at their estate in Bucks County. Billed as a charity fundraiser for* Environment For Tomorrow, *it costs more to put on than it raises in contributions. The Gibsons, however, feel it's a good way to promote their pet cause, as well as reinforce their own considerable clout. The elite meet, connections are made, cameras record the goings on for the entertainment of the mere mortals among us, and everyone, in the end, is beholden to the Walter Gibsons.*

On the day after the gala, as is her custom, Nan discreetly hands over a personal check for one million dollars, in addition to the check representing raised funds, to the director of the EFT at their headquarters in lower Manhattan. Nan's a loyal volunteer who shows up every Tuesday without fail, to do whatever needs to be done – answer phones, run errands, address mailings. Nothing is beneath her, and she gets no special treatment. The staff all call her Mrs. G. Most of them know she's somebody special, but they're just too tired to care. They appreciate her because she's nice and a hard worker, and that's just how she likes it. Only the director knows about the annual donation. No one else needs to.

Nan has always understood her fortunate position in life and the responsibilities that come with that position. She was born to it, as Nancy Dalton, eldest daughter of the Thatcher Daltons of Boston. Her father, the renowned department store magnate, believed in "Giving thanks, giving back, and never giving up." He sent his children to public school, put them to work after school in one of his stores when they were sixteen, helped them invest their modest earnings so they could learn the value of money, and advised them in choosing worthy causes to support. His expectations were great, but his heart was greater. He loved his three girls and beamed with pride at the mention of one of their names.

Joanna, the baby of the family, was the wild child who became a Lady. Fun, spontaneous and full of life, she was on her third husband before she was twenty five. The first two are vague memories, but the last was an English Lord forty years her senior, who, in spite of the age difference was her great love. Lord Spencer died in his sleep just two years after they were married. Contrary to popular belief, he left her only debts and a title. She settled the first and savored the last. Lady Jo never married again, though she was rarely without consort. She devoted her title, her considerable energy and larger-than-life personality to children's causes the world over.

Katherine, the middle child was the most gifted academically and truly the most beautiful. She grew up to become an internationally respected archaeologist who sat on the boards of several museums, giving generously to those museums from her personal trust. Highly sought after as a social presence, Kit, as she was known to friends and family, eschewed married life saying, "With the notable exception of my father, it's been my experience that men are easier to appreciate when they've been dead for 400 years. Much better company, too."

As impressive as Kit Dalton and Lady Jo Spencer were, it was their sister Nan who achieved true icon status. Not as beautiful as Kit, not as provocative as Jo, Nan had always been noted for her undeniable grace and natural elegance. Confident, charming, charismatic, she radiated health and wit; she had never taken a backward step.

Nan always knew she was her father's favorite; and she, in turn, worshipped the ground he walked on. She wanted to make him proud; do right by him. When she felt the time had come for her to marry, Nan went in search of a man like her father and found him in Walter Gibson. Same goodness, same generosity, same Puritan work ethic, same enormous success. Together they became the most powerful of power couples – a benefactorial dynamic duo working for good under the guise of capitalist royalty. Her father would have been proud.

Somewhere in the apartment a phone rings, interrupting Nan's thoughts. She's out on the terrace overlooking Central Park, having her morning tea.

"Excuse me, Mrs. Gibson, Mr. Patrik is calling to confirm your 1:00 lunch date at *Endive*. Do you wish to speak with him?" It's Laura, her assistant.

"Yes...no...I'm sorry, Laura, my mind is somewhere else. Please tell Mr. Patrik 1:00 is fine. I'll meet him there."

"Yes, ma'am," Laura paused at the doorway. "Is everything all right, Mrs. Gibson?"

Nan smiled at her mother hen reassuringly. They'd been together for twenty years. Nothing escaped her. Sensitive to Nan's every inflection, she instinctively knew when to intrude and when not to. She also knew how to telegraph her concern without being invasive – a fine quality, that.

"Yes, dear, everything's fine. I'm just going to sit a while longer and enjoy this beautiful morning."

Laura closed the terrace doors. Nan was once again alone with her thoughts.

Last year's Summer Solstice Gala *– a beautiful night, a beautiful crowd. Ricky London's Band played Cole Porter while the guests danced and posed and enjoyed seeing and being seen. Everyone was someone at this party; young, old, famous, infamous. Nan enjoyed* *compiling the guest list for her big night, mixing it up and throwing in a few surprises. This year she had included a new pop star of the moment – a sweet young thing who, no doubt, would be old news by this time next year; but right now, she was everything. The teen queen had arrived wearing a little Versace nothing. She was noticed.*

It was well into the evening when Nan finally had a chance to catch up with Becka and Victor Conrad. They were sitting at one of the tables by the pool enjoying a laugh with Shawn Patrik and his date for the evening, Natalie Parker, the former movie queen.

"This appears to be the fun table," said Nan as she approached them, "What did I miss?' Victor stood, offering Nan his chair. She patted his arm, "No, please. I'm afraid if I sit down, I won't get up."

"That's what I said an hour ago," said Natalie, "and it turned out to be true." They all laughed. "But the champagne and caviar keep coming this way, so I'm in no hurry. Fabulous party, Nan."

"Thank you, Natalie. We're always so pleased when you can join us." And she meant it. Natalie was a glamorous, down-to-earth, warm, wonderful woman. Her reality surpassed her legend in every respect.

"Natalie was just telling us the best story about going to McDonald's for the first time," said Shawn, taking Nan's hand as he did so.

"Well, I'd never been, you see, and I always wondered what the fuss was about. I'm afraid we created something of a scene."

"We?" asked Nan.

"Yes. Angela, Rhonda and yours truly. Lunch with the girls, don'tcha know?"

"You gotta love it," said Shawn, "Three goddesses of the silver screen decked out, I imagine, in full diva drag..." he turned to Natalie, "You <u>did</u> wear the big diamonds, didn't you?"

"I always dress for lunch, Sweet, you know that."

Nan smiled at the mental picture. "So, how was it?" she asked.

"I had the Big Mac," said Natalie, toying with one of her rings, "and you know, it was very good."

Laughter echoed in the air as the fun table was joined by Carla Montgomery and a very handsome, very young man.

"Nan," she said, "Glorious evening."

"Carla. Beautiful as always," then turning to her escort, "I'm sorry, I thought I knew everyone here."

Carla did the introductions. "Nan, this is Leo Ventura, a marvelous, new talent. Leo, this is our hostess, Nan Gibson."

Leo bowed slightly and said, "Mrs. Gibson, it's an honor to meet you. Thank you for allowing me to be a part of your special evening."

So like a little boy, she thought. And so handsome. She shook his hand and said, "Do you know, Mr. Ventura, I used to be impressed by over-achievers, but they're so easy to come by. Now I'm impressed by people of any age who are well-mannered. They're very rare. Delighted to meet you."

"Leo Ventura!" Shawn had stood up from his chair to greet him. "Everyone, this is Leo Ventura. Say hello."

They all did as they were requested.

Nan saw that neither Victor nor Becka had taken their eyes off Carla, even as they said hello to the young man, and what very different expressions their faces revealed. She knew, of course, about Carla's and Victor's affair; had known since just after the Met gala. And Shawn had recently filled her in about the end of the affair, due, apparently, to Carla's lack of interest. It seems the wizard of Wall Street was not magic in the boudoir, and our Miss Montgomery bores easily. Poor Victor, though. He seemed to have fallen for her and was contemplating divorce when Carla let him know – via text – that they were done.

Becka had known about her husband's affair all along and couldn't have cared less; but, now that he had been unceremoniously dumped for this young, albeit handsome, nobody, she was furious. It was as if she'd been insulted because her husband wasn't worth Carla Montgomery's time, and that reflected badly on her.

Nan felt for Victor. Judging from his expression, he still cared for Carla and wanted her back, poor fool. Judging from Becka's expression, she just wanted Carla gone, the sooner the better. Carla, for her part, seemed not to notice.

Meanwhile, Natalie only had eyes for Leo. Patting Shawn's empty chair she said, "Why don't you come sit by me and tell me all about this talent of yours." As Natalie and Leo proceeded to enjoy a lively discussion, Becka spoke up.

"Victor, I'd like to dance. Now." She got up, brushing past Carla as she stepped away from the table. Victor also stood. He touched Carla's elbow as he stepped by her, looking sadly and longingly into her eyes. Carla smiled back at him with an empty, anonymous smile, as if he were a valet offering to check on her car. Watching the Conrad's walk away, Shawn said, "Is anyone else feeling chilly?"

"What was that about?" asked Nan, knowing full well.

"I have no idea," said Carla.

"A word of advice, darling, if I may," said Nan, "be careful, the enemies you make and be careful the hearts you break."

"Listen to her, sweetie," said Shawn, "you wouldn't want to wake up one morning and find out you've been killed by a vengeful lover or jealous spouse, would you? Messy. Very messy."

Carla laughed, "Thank you both for your touching concern, but I'll be fine. I can take care of myself. And now I have Leo to take care of me, too."

"At least until tomorrow," added Shawn sarcastically.

Nan slipped her arm around Carla's waist, like sisters, and said, "Just take care, that's all we're saying, in our very different ways. You're cold and callous and completely without morals, but we should miss you terribly if you weren't here," they brushed cheeks and kissed the air, "and with that, I suppose I should tend to my other guests. Hugs to you all. Enjoy the champagne."

How glib, thought Nan. How lighter than air and totally without content. And wasn't that usually the way with their crowd? God forbid any conversation existed that wasn't meant to impress or meant to amuse. She was just as guilty as the rest, possibly even more so. She set the rules, after all.

Of course the rationale was that this is evening fun we're talking about, and we all have such exhausting, serious days. While that's certainly true for some, it doesn't hold true for most. Maybe the air's too thin up here in the penthouse world to sustain a profound thought or sincere emotion. Or maybe we just don't care about each other, It's such a bother after all.

Oh, enough with the self loathing, she said to herself. There's a need for this social display and as long as you coax them along, the lemmings can be eased into doing good without their even knowing it. Thank heavens you have Walter, who constantly reminds you that it's a job like any other; and Shawn, who sees the players for whom they really are. No, you're doing fine. Father would still be proud. Concentrate on the big picture,he would say. Concentrate on the end results. And remember, we're all doing the best we can.

But what was Carla doing, really? What was she about? So much better and so much worse than all the rest. She made her own rules and broke them freely; and we all stood by and watched. And now she's gone. Killed by one of us.

They say that hot air rises to the top, but I don't think that's true at all. I think it's the cold air in this rarified atmosphere. Yes, I think it's the icy, unfeeling cold.

29. See and Be Seen

No thank you, I'll stand.

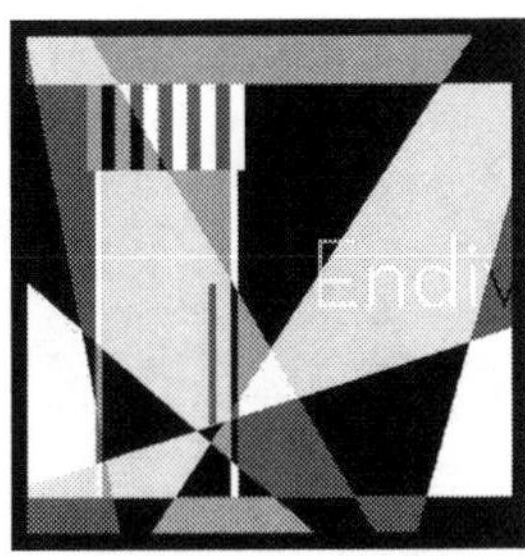

At five minutes to one, Nan steps into *Endive*, the latest must-see-and-be-seen restaurant just off Park Avenue on 53rd. The room is filled with a lunchtime clientele of carefully styled ladies-who-shop and the occasional Zegna-clad gentleman joining his polished wife or trophy mistress for a quick bite between cut-throat wheelings and dealings. In her standard afternoon attire of white oxford cloth men's shirt, trim khaki slacks, Ferragamo flats, and a favorite scarf thrown casually over one arm, no make-up to speak of and no jewelry save her daytime Cartier tank and her wedding band, Nan is easily and naturally the chic-est woman in the room. People stare, conversations stop. She returns the wave from this one and the smile from that one.

Nan hates restaurants like *Endive*, hates the whole idea of going to lunch. She much prefers her tuna-on-whole-wheat and iced coffee standing at the kitchen counter. Delicious and done, in no time at all, then on with the business of the day. Don't these women have lives? Don't they have things they need, or better yet, want to do?

But she is here today at Shawn's request. He had chosen *Endive* because it's a restaurant he had designed; and knowing how rarely Nan ventures out to dine, he wanted her to see it. It was a wonderful environment, she would tell him. The walls are lacquered a pale yellow-green and the tables, small and intimately arranged, are crisply covered in mint green linen. The chairs, Chinese Chippendale, are white with leather cushions of robin's egg blue. The bleached wood floors have been stenciled in an intricate Moroccan tile design. Light is generous but soft; background music is minimalist and soothing. Very nice.

"You like?" It's Shawn. He's just arrived and has quietly stepped to her side.

"It's a beautiful room, Shawny."

"Made all the more beautiful by your presence." He takes her arm and kisses her on the cheek.

"Thanks for coming. I know how you hate the lunch thing."

"I won't deny it. But this is lovely to see. Is the food any good?"

"Overdressed salads that look like hats."

"Is it exorbitant?"

"Ridiculously so."

"Now that I've seen it, do we have to stay?"

"There's a *Burger Haven* across the street."

"Perfect."

"Let's go."

As Nan Gibson and Shawn Patrik leave *Endive*, a wave of insecurity washes over the remaining patrons – *Is there a newer restaurant? A better restaurant? Where are they going and why don't we know? I could die, I could just die...*

30. Adam and Eve on a Raft

What's good here?

Once settled into their rustic wooden booth, complete with relish container and paper napkin dispenser, these two pillars of society, these two style-setting, chic sophisticates, proceed to order bacon burgers, medium rare, and lite beers, with a side of onion rings, please.

"I was thinking about Carla this morning," said Nan.

"I've been thinking of nothing else." Shawn's eyes, which had been avoiding Nan's, make contact. They were puffy and very tired. "I feel like I've lost my twin."

Nan reaches across the table and holds Shawn's hands in her own. He gives her a quick flicker of a smile and continues. "I had a visit from the police this morning. A Detective Maroney. He came with Able Ryder, of all people."

"Able? Really?"

"Yes. Funny, I know. Able, of course, knew Carla and explained that he was assisting the detective in his investigation. Maybe the detective was having a little trouble communicating with our crowd. I don't blame him. I often have that problem myself. I know Able; not well, but I've run into him several times over the years. Did you know he once dated Carla? Yes, I know. You're thinking, *"Who didn't?"* He folds and unfolds his hands again and again.

Nan watches her fragile friend with motherly concern.

"Anyway," he continues, "Able did make the whole thing much easier, less offensive. They were, after all, asking if I had an alibi, and if I had any idea who did this. And I don't, Nan. Honest to God, I don't. Yes, she was difficult. Yes, she was a bitch sometimes. She had enemies; we all do. But not like this. Nothing like this. It doesn't make sense..."

Shawn is playing with a speck of salt, pushing it around with his knife.

"I think the detective is hoping for a jilted lover scenario, but I explained to him that one of Carla's great gifts was her ability to handle men, even after she was through with them. Look at Victor. He was completely in love with her, even ready to divorce Becka. And Carla was terrible to him. But he still continued to -- what's the word --*appreciate* her, long after their story was over. Able agreed with me. He said that Carla dropped him cold, but he never even disliked her because she was completely up front and disarmingly honest. And it's true, she was, which is why I'm so confused, because what if she wasn't? What if there was another side to her that even I didn't know? And what if she was in some sort of danger and knew it and couldn't even tell me?"

"Shawn, Carla loved you, probably more than she loved anyone or anything; but she was a complicated, aggressively manipulative woman. Of course, she had secrets. Of course, there were sides to her that none of us knew. I think that was always part of her allure. I adored Carla, found her fascinating, but I don't think I ever knew her, not really."

The waiter arrives with their order. "That was two bacon cheese, two Bud lites and a basket of rings. Have everything you need?"

"Yes thank you," says Nan, looking over at Shawn, "I think we'll be fine." She lifts her beer and motions for him to do the same. "To absent friends," she says and touches his bottle with her own.

"Shawn, do you remember last Summer Solstice?" Nan asks, looking remarkably elegant as she takes a bite from her very unwieldy burger. "That's what I was thinking about earlier today. You and Natalie were sitting by the pool with the Conrads when Carla came by with her newest young man..."

"Leo Ventura. You saw how the newspapers had a field day with him, painting him as the killer, not even bothering to find out if he had an alibi, which he did. Madness. It's all madness. I know Leo. He's a good kid. And not stupid. He didn't mistake his relationship with Carla for anything other than what it was. They were friends. Bed buddies. And he appreciated what she was doing for him – educating him, showing him a better life, helping him build a career..."

"Yes, I'm sure he did." she interrupts, attempting to lighten the mood a little, "He's a very polite boy, as I recall. And not unattractive. I wouldn't be surprised if Carla had been more smitten with him than he with her."

Shawn smiles at last, "Everybody loves Leo Ventura." He took a sip of his beer. "Do you remember Natalie's reaction to meeting Leo?"

"Dear Natalie. May she never change," Nan dabs at the corners of her mouth with a napkin,"But what keeps reappearing in my mind, what first appeared moments after hearing of Carla's death, wasn't Mr. Ventura, but Becka and her expression when Carla joined the table. She was seething and became, quite suddenly, hideous with rage."

"Becka hated Carla from the first time they met; everything about her, but mostly the disdain, I think. The way she could be so cordially icy to her, women in general for that matter. Except you, of course. Carla always admired and respected you."

"Admired, yes. Respected? I don't think so. I was one of the blueprints she used in her personal renovation. Becka, of course, is exactly the same, but not as bright, much more transparent and much less interesting. Carla, as you said, was nothing if not honest. She told me once, that she had tried to seduce Walter – you probably already know this – and he laughed, thanked her for the compliment and sent her on her way," Nan smiles, thinking of her husband, "The next day, she phoned and said, in so many words, that she could have any man she wanted, so why had she failed with Walter, and, realizing it must have something to do with me, wanted to know my secret? Pure Carla when you think of it, asking the wife why she couldn't break up her marriage."

"What did you tell her?"

"Something about love, honor and cherish, which, naturally, she had trouble understanding."

"But you never held it against her."

"A waste of time and effort. Suffice it to sat she was a charming, beautiful, intelligent dinner companion and she made me laugh. Sometimes that's enough. Becka on the other hand is, how shall I put this, not as secure in her marriage as I am in mine: and Carla threatened that union."

"But Victor's and Carla's affair had ended."

"His infatuation hadn't, and that's what I saw the night of the Summer Solstice. Victor still loved Carla and Becka knew it. The following week, Becka and I met up at the museum – a committee meeting to begin planning the next costume exhibit. We were having coffee before the meeting began, chatting about, oh, I don't know, the weather, theater, you possibly, when she casually brought up Carla's name in conversation. I asked if they'd made peace and she said to me, 'The only peace I'll have with Carla is after she's dead and buried.'"

And pause...

"You don't honestly think that Becka Conrad went to Carla's apartment, killed her with a, what, a letter opener, a nail file, then, a few hours later, showed up at your Audubon thing in Bucks as if nothing had happened, and no one was the wiser? I was there. You were there, too, Nan. You saw her. Becka's not that good an actress. She's transparent. You said so yourself."

"I know you're right."

"Of course I am," he replies. But neither one is really sure.

31. Up to Speed

And then that happened.

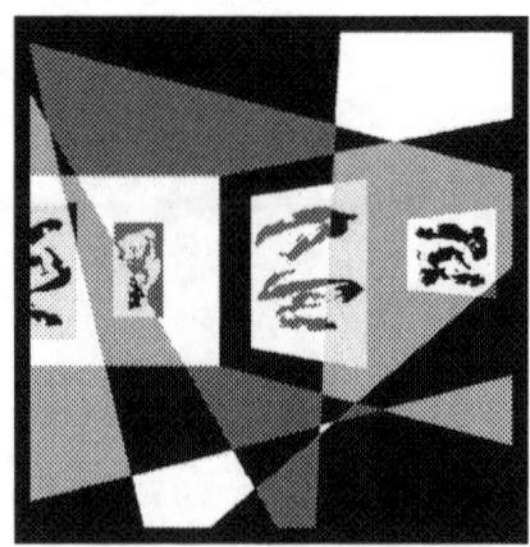

"So, how goes the investigation?" Hugo Swann asks, as he pays the delivery boy for our lunch.

"I'm only helping out. You know, Hugo, I don't know if I should be pissed off at you or thank you for giving Detective Maroney my name. This is a weird bunch of people, the people in Carla's world...our world."

"You're just figuring that out?"

"No, of course not. It's just that it seems the more I learn about them, the less I know. Especially Carla."

"I know what you mean. She was in and out of here all the time, and we saw each other at shows and openings pretty often, but, well, I don't even feel sad about her death. I don't feel anything at all. I'm not even surprised it happened, if you want to know the truth."

"Exactly! I mean, I want to feel badly. I think I should feel badly. We slept together, for Christ's sake. But I don't. And you know what? Nobody else does either, not that we've talked to, anyway."

"Who have you talked to?"

"We started with the family...whoa, talk about a long day's journey into Bryn Mawr."

"That bad? I only know Sidney. She seems cool, no?"

"Well, not in her mother's house. I like Sidney, but I never saw this side of her before – mean, sarcastic, *better than*. And the brother, Thorne, just takes up space. But Cassandra – Mom – now that's a piece of work. All kinds of perfect on the outside, but inside, a mystery; and I realized, as I was watching her...like mother, like eldest daughter. That's exactly how Carla would have turned out. Beautiful, classy, smart, richer than God, and bored, so bored by everything and everyone. But keeping up the facade because, well, that's what one does. You know what? I don't think they even care that she was murdered. I think it's just an inconvenience, something they have to deal with."

This week's business lunch is at Hugo's desk in his office at the gallery. Hugo's assistant, Tess Weaver, is out front, busily typing away at her computer and answering the occasional phone call. Tess, with her master's in 20th Century Art from NYU and her doctorate in American Painting from Yale; Tess, with her remarkable memory and eye for detail; Tess, with her opaque tights and miniskirt kilts; her shiny, swingy hair and incandescent skin; Tess, who could have had any one of a thousand prestige jobs, but instead offered her overqualified services to Hugo Swann; Tess, who, at 26, still believed it was all about the talent and not about the deal. That's sweet.

She raps on the glass wall separating Hugo's office from the main gallery. "Excuse me, Hugo, Kate just phoned and asked me to tell you that she's on her way. Also Miss Vesprey confirmed her 5:00 appointment. I'm going across the street to get a latte, if that's o.k. Be right back."

"Sure, take your time. Oh, and Tess? While you're at it...eat something?"

"Hugo," she says impatiently but affectionately, as if she's talking to her Aunt Helen, "I had a muffin this morning. I'm fine. And, no, I'm not anorexic, no, I'm not bulimic. I'm just thin! All right? Now, finish your own lunch. I'll be back in a minute."

She turns and walks across the gallery, stepping out into the early afternoon sun, barely casting a shadow. Hugo follows her every move.

"The daughter you never had?" I ask.

"Something like that."

"Tess is a great girl. You could do a lot worse. Come to think of it, you always do a lot worse."

"Like you said, she's a girl. A very young girl," he drums his fingers on his water bottle, "Anyway. Back to the Chase Montgomerys."

"Right. Well, that's about it for them, as of now. Dad was a no-show, so we're going back to talk with him this week. Detective Jerry wants to re-interview the other three separately, Cassandra at home, probably, and the kiddies – anyplace but. That'll be this week, too. The sooner, the better.

"I was also along when he interviewed Shawn. And yesterday, we met with Leo Ventura at his studio. Nice guy. Not what I expected. The papers painted a picture of this louche, gigolo type, but he doesn't come off that way at all. He's kind of, I don't know...sweet."

"Detective Jerry? And the knife artist is sweet?"

"Yeah. How about that? Oh, the paintings are for shit. Have you ever seen them? Way too much angst, all show. It's Julian Schnabel all over again." I shudder at the thought.

Hugo laughs. "Carla sent me a few slides of his work. Pretty dreadful. I told her to try the Chesterfield. They would probably be interested, if only because of their size. And they *are* big. And dark and dreary and immature, but you know, in the right room..."

"Spare me. Anyway, I did like the kid. He was truly sad when he spoke about Carla. He cared for her, and yes, they were sleeping together; but he knew it wasn't a serious romance to her. Or to him, for that matter. He was very mature about that. He said she was his tutor and, I guess, champion. She taught him more about art than any teacher he'd ever had. She even gave him homework."

"How so?"

"She told him he couldn't go off into abstract neverland until he knew more about the periods that made abstraction possible. So she gave him books to read; not the boring textbooks, but the juicy biographies of the famous dead guys. And she had him copy different artists, from Ingres to Jasper Johns, so he could experience, first-hand, the challenge and the reward of creating. The thing is, what she apparently could see is, Ventura's genuinely talented, bludgeoned canvases aside. Technically, he's very facile. He can mimic any number of styles. He showed us some collage pieces he had done, and I'm telling you, if I didn't know they weren't Matisse, I wouldn't know they weren't Matisse. Then he showed us a Vermeer, then a Bonnard, and on and on. It was impressive."

"Are you saying these are forgeries?" Hugo looked concerned.

"Not really. He's copying the image, not the ageing process or the exact materials or the proper dimensions. It's the way they used to do it at the Philadelphia Academy."

"And still, with all that inherent talent, he chooses to stab defenseless canvases and call it art."

"These kids today. What're you gonna do? I think he's trying to find his own voice, as it were. Even Carla told him gimmicks are an easier sell than traditional painting, representational or abstract; and you and I both know that's true. I blame Jeff Koons."

The artist, famous for displaying basketballs in aquariums, vacuum cleaners on pedestals and electroplated inflatable bunny rabbits, irritated the hell out of Able.

"You can't blame Jeff Koons. Blame the people who buy Jeff Koons. Certainly nobody knew more about promotion in the art world than Carla, so if she thought she could make Ventura a main event, I guess she could. Stranger things have happened."

"Yesterday, as a matter of fact. While we were still at Leo Ventura's studio, he got a phone call from the Bentley-Shiff offering him a one-man show. His first. That was followed by a phone call from *Focus*, the tv news show with the blonde who's married to what's-his-name.

They want to do a profile on Leo and his work. They're calling it – can you guess? – *Leo the Knife*."

"Unbelievable."

"All too believable, I'd say."

32. A Cut Above the Rest

Everyone's a critic.

When Tess returns moments later, she's accompanied by Kate. They had run into, each other at the Starbucks across the street. Tess is intently listening to Kate, who is slicing the air with her free hand, apparently illustrating her story. Still gesturing dramatically as they cross the gallery to Hugo's office, Kate concludes by saying, "...an awful way to go, but whoever it was, apparently showed some mercy."

"Mocha frappuccino?" I ask.

"Of course," replies Kate as she leans over to kiss Hugo, "It's the coffee for people who hate coffee. Hi boys. Miss me?"

"Always," says Hugo.

Kate turns to me now and kisses me on the forehead. "I was just telling Tess what I now know about death by stabbing."

"That's my girl. Always so good at small talk."

"It's really very interesting," says Tess, "Where did you learn all of this?"

"At my gynecologist's this morning."

"Eeeww," Hugo and I whine in unison.

Kate looks at Tess. "You can sense the testosterone, can't you? Relax boys. I was in the waiting room. Waiting, before my exam. And even though Dr. Freddy is one of Park Avenue's finest, his reading material dates back to Gutenberg."

"You call your gynecologist Dr. Freddy?"

"Able."

"Sorry...you were saying?"

"I was leafing through the *Sunday Times Arts and Liesure* section when I came across an article by Carla Montgomery. It took me by surprise for obvious reasons. I checked the date on the newspaper and saw it was four years old. The article was a glowing profile of her then new discovery, Bobby Tyler. Blah-blah-blah, genius-genius-genius. Typical Montgomery. Then I saw, right next to it, an article about an exhibition of knives and swords at The Japan Society; and I thought, now isn't that ironic? Just then, the doctor –"

"Dr. Freddy?" asked Able.

"Yes, Dr. Freddy," she pauses," you know I hate you right now."

"Just right now, You'll love me again in a minute."

"Doubtful...as I was saying, Dr. Freddy was standing next to me, reading over my shoulder, and he said, 'Now there's a bad cosmic joke for you. We got to talking about the murder, and he said that stabbing is a particularly awful way to die because it's like surgery without an anesthetic and it takes so long to bleed out. I told him that I was aiding in the investigation – he was very impressed – and I'd heard she died quickly. He said that her throat must have been slashed."

"Aiding in the investigation? A slight exaggeration."

Kate sneers at me. Literally sneers at me.

"Dr. Freddy thinks I'm utterly fascinating and capable of anything. He would be right." She sips her non-coffee, "Okay, so maybe I exaggerated a little...as I was saying, apparently there are basically two kinds of people who use knives as murder weapons. Impulse killers use them because they're cheap, like pocket knives, or readily available, like kitchen knives. They just hack away in a blind rage. The results are really messy and more often than not, the victim lives but sustains internal injuries that could be life threatening later on, as well as some pretty horrific scarring.

"The other kind of knife wielder is an obsessive/compulsive, analytical perfectionist type who has done his homework, knows where the key targets are, purposely wants to mar the surface of his victim, finds a strange, choreographic beauty to the actual movements involved and also enjoys the finality of slashing the throat, which not only guarantees a quick death if done properly, but also guarantees a quiet one. The victim can't scream.

"Dr. Freddy says this perfectionist type sometimes does the throat thing because it allows them to feel merciful and godlike, as if they're putting this poor wretch out of his, or her, misery."

"Even though they're the one that caused the misery," interjects Tess.

"Exactly. It's a very intimate way to kill somebody. You have to be embracing, basically. So all the emotions come flooding together. Love. Hate. Rage. Jealousy."

"And they run hot and cold at the same time," said Able, "So, if I hear you right, you're saying whoever killed Carla cared for her as much as they hated her?"

"Right."

"So we can rule out the people who just hated her, because this was too...um... thoughtful a killing?" I say...uncomfortably, I might add.

"Maybe not thoughtful, but certainly thought-filled," Kate replies. "Didn't we just sound like an episode of *NCIS*?"

"Good work, Detective Lindsey," says I.

"Thank you, Detective Ryder," says she.

"Very impressive," says Hugo, "but I have a question. Why does your gynecologist know so much about knife killing?"

"Before he decided to become a gynecologist, Dr. Freddy was thinking of becoming a criminal psychologist. Obviously, he changed his mind; and speaking for the ladies of New York, we are most appreciative."

"Handsome?" asks Tess.

"You have no idea," says Kate with a sigh. "So Able, when are we meeting Detective Jerry? I want to impress him with what I've learned today."

"We're meeting him at 2:30. That only gives us 45 minutes. We'd better get moving."

"The investigation continues?" asks Hugo.

"Yes. We get to pry into the lives of Victor and Becka Conrad this afternoon."

"I've had dealings with Becka Conrad. I don't think she's a very kind person," says Tess.

Hugo looks at her warmly, "What Tess means is, Becka Conrad's a black belt bitch. "Didn't you do her portrait a little while back? The husband too, right?" asks Hugo.

"Yes. Thanks to Shawn. The husband, Victor, was a breeze. Nice guy. We laughed a lot. She, on the other hand, was difficult from the get-go. She's very condescending, not too knowledgable, and completely self-absorbed."

"Sounds like my manicurist," said Kate.

"Perhaps," says Hugo, "but your manicurist isn't married to a Wall Street king and friends with Nan Gibson and Shawn Patrick. Ms. Conrad relies heavily on her connections and hides behind them whenever it's necessary. Her husband, by contrast, couldn't care less about all that. He's a great guy. You'll like him."

"I hope not too much," says Kate, "he might be our killer!"

I look up and around into the corners of the room, with my hand held up to my ear.

"What are you doing?" asks Kate as she reapplies her lipstick.

"Listening for the soundtrack."

She throws her lipstick back in her Fendi clutch, snaps it shut, then looks at me as if I'm a telemarketer. "Remind me later why I tolerate you?"

"Will do."

33. Make Book on It

A little bird told me.

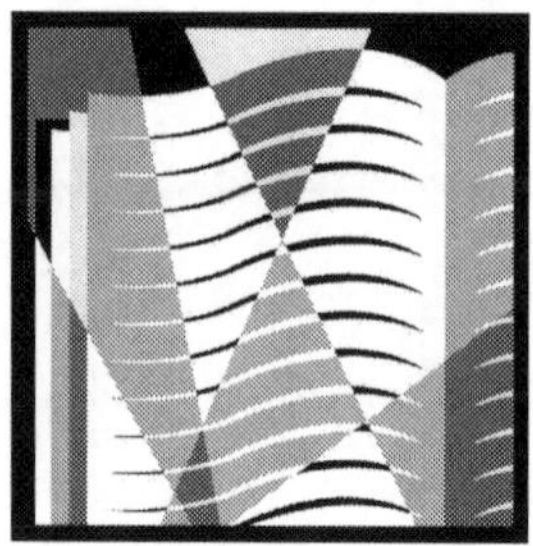

Karen Richards sits at her desk and stares out the window. A pigeon, a large grey pigeon, stands on the ledge contemplating his next move. Would he venture out, take flight into the air of possibilities? Or would he hold his ground, safe and secure? Watching. Waiting.

Another pigeon, smaller and a light creamy color, touches down on the same ledge. A few quick nods of both their heads and just like that, creamy pigeon takes off, followed in short order by grey pigeon.

Isn't that just like a man, Karen thinks, to throw caution to the wind at the first nod from a dirty blonde.

Karen turns away from the window and back to her desk. She opens the bottom drawer and pulls out her bag. Searching inside among the mints and sunglasses, lipsticks and credit card receipts, she finds her cigarettes. She tells everyone she's quitting, but that's never gonna happen. The rules are, if she wants to smoke, she has to go outside of the building. But Karen Richards is not one to follow the rules. You don't survive as a literary agent in New York by following the rules. You flirt, bribe, coax, lie, do whatever is necessary to get a client and keep a client. You build egos, forge alliances, wage wars. And you smoke if you want to. You smoke.

Karen lights one of her cigarettes, sits back and takes a deep drag. She looks at the manuscript sitting front and center on her desk. She reads the cover sheet – *Picture Perfect: An Unveiling of My Art-Filled Life by Carla Montgomery.*

The manuscript had just arrived on Friday, by messenger. Karen took it home with her over the weekend and read it. The book is juicy, sexy and scandal-filled, with more than its share of secrets and disclosures. It's well-written, a good read, and has a famously beautiful celebrity as its subject. It was gold.

And now, the subject-slash-author is dead. Even better.

Karen Richards had been Carla Montgomery's literary agent for the last five years. They'd been introduced by a mutual friend at the Times. *Carla had told the friend she was looking for an agent. Karen had told the friend she thought Carla was ready for books. A meeting was arranged. Brunch at Balthazar. The two women disliked each other on site, but recognized a shared play-to-win attitude. They sized each other up and dressed each other down, alternating the roles of interviewer and interviewee. In the end, they respected each other's talents, were impressed by each other's intellect. And still disliked each other enormously.*

But this was about business, not friendship. There was money to be made, and there were goals to be achieved. The two women knew they could be a formidable team. And so, five years, five books and three best-sellers later, Carla Montgomery is a recognized literary star, thanks to Karen Richard's guidance. Quite a feat, since Carla isn't a movie star, rock idol or former lawyer, and her books are basically art history text books, certainly not main stream fare. But the Carla Karen pitched was special, different from the rest. Her column was in the Times *every weekend and the* New Yorker *every month, thereby supplying a captive audience and a recognizable cool factor. Also, she was known as much for her beauty as for her brain, which made her the ideal talk-show circuit guest.*

Karen negotiated the deals, changing publishers along the way. She was involved in every aspect of promotion and marketing, and had demanded from the first that Carla's face appear on the cover of every book. She had convinced the powers-that-be that Carla had crossover appeal. She proved to be right.

As Carla's books became more and more successful, Karen asked for more and more of everything, for her client and herself. Bigger advances, higher royalties, more perks, more gimmies. She usually got what she asked for.

It had been Karen's idea for Carla to do the autobiography. There was a growing curiosity among her fans about Carla's own story. And Karen knew the story was a good one. But she had no idea how good and no idea that Carla would tell so much. In writing her own story, Carla exposed the lives and peculiarities of everyone with whom she came in contact. It was a no-holds-barred vendetta disguised as an intimate acknowledgement of her personal journey – not always pretty, but always so very interesting, don't you think?

Carla openly wrote about her very active love life, naming famous names and their unique proclivities. Chapters were devoted to the unseemly and unethical machinations of the art world, alluding to the involvement of society's elite. Forgeries were implied, fortunes were questioned, thefts were assumed, suicides were inferred.

Karen was alternately shocked at the revelations and thrilled at the impending media event such a book would become. And now, to make the timing even more perfect, more potent, Carla had gone and gotten herself killed. Having now read the manuscript, Karen could think of any number of people who would be more than happy to see Carla dead. It was a mystery who had killed her. It wasn't a mystery that someone might have wanted her dead.

Karen reaches for her remaining cigarette, lights it and takes a long drag, exhaling slowly and enjoying the moment. In the end, she thinks to herself, Carla had set the stage for her own murder. She had arrived on the scene – beautiful, desirable – and had used everyone she'd ever known as a stepping stone to her own glory. She had flirted, bribed, coaxed, and lied. She had done whatever was necessary. But in the end, in the light of day, she was just another dirty blonde.

34. Nouveau is Better than No Riche at All

Don't forget to remove the tags.

"Hello Able, Detective Maroney, Ms. Lindsey, I'm Becka Conrad. Please do come in."

She's pretty, and precise to a painful extreme. A carefully executed paint-by-number copy of a dazzling original, the original being Nan Gibson twenty years ago. She's a fine mimic, a good imitation; but she is not now, and never will be the equal of Nan Gibson. She has the grace and the style, the words and the music; but something's missing. Oh, right... a soul.

"Thank you for seeing us, Mrs. Conrad," says Detective Jerry. "We'll try not to take up too much of your time."

"Anything to help, detective. Why don't we talk in the living room," she motions to her right as she turned toward her left, "I'll tell my husband you're here."

The tap of Becka's shoes against the marble floor is the only sound in the quiet, museum-like apartment. It's completely, severely white, punctuated by large, important looking abstract paintings. There's nothing soft in this environment, nothing personal. It has been designed for impact and, on that level, succeeds brilliantly. But I'm afraid to speak for fear of an echo, and I think I can see my breath...

"Cozy, don't you think?" asks Kate.

"Where do you suppose the Christmas tree goes?"

"In someone else's apartment."

Detective Jerry smiles in spite of himself. As Kate and I try to get situated on one of the low-slung, wafer-thin sofas upholstered in crisp, white linen, I think it might be safer to stand.

Once again, the sound of high heels on marble can be heard coming towards us. We look to the entryway to see an Armani ad come to life. Victor Conrad is as handsome as his wife is pretty, but with a noticeable, almost tangible, air of sadness. Becka holds on to his arm in a way that shows she doesn't do it often. But today she's in presentation mode. The Conrads have arrived.

Introductions are made, and everyone is seated. Everyone, except Detective Jerry.

"Able, good to see you again. I'm sorry it has to be under these circumstances," Victor said kindly, sincerely.

"Yes Able. So sad." says Becka, as if she just realized we actually knew each other. "We just saw you the other week at the Audubon event, yes?"

"Yes. I was there with Kate," I say, motioning towards Kate.

"Of course, Ms. Lindsey. Welcome to our home," she replies in Kate's direction.

"Your home is beautiful, Mrs. Conrad," she offers.

"Thank you. Shawn Patrik helped me design the space. We find the order very comforting, our lives are so chaotic," her lips smile but her eyes do not. 'Mean Girl,' thinks Kate.

Now, she turns her attention to me. "Able, you've come to speak with us about Carla, isn't that so? A terrible thing. Carla was so vital, so full of life. It's a tragedy to have all of that talent and beauty destroyed so brutally."

Her husband looks at her as if she's speaking in another language, one he's never heard before.

"Carla and I were very close," Becka continues. She notices everyone's expressions of surprise, subtle though they may have been, and proceeds, seeming to enjoy her own performance.

"Everyone thought we loathed each other, I'm sure that's what you've heard, but it simply wasn't true. Carla and I shared many passions. Art, design, fashion..."

"Your husband," interrupts Kate.

Victor doesn't respond at all. He's seated by his wife, but his thoughts are elsewhere. Becka glares at Kate with utter contempt. Kate meets her gaze and lobs it back.
Becka turns to me and smiles with a practiced insincerity, "It's true, she loved Victor. Everyone does. My husband is a very desirable man..." – still no response from Victor – "... and yes, they had an affair. But that was ages ago. It was really my fault. Victor and I had been having problems, mundane married people's problems..." as she says this, Becka looks briefly and icily at Kate. "...and he went to Carla for comfort. Carla was only trying to be a friend. She couldn't help it if she fell in love with my husband," She strokes his arm in a weak imitation of affection. "When Victor and I reconciled, Carla graciously stepped aside and all was forgiven. Unfortunately, our circle loves gossip. And I see Ms. Lindsey does also."

"I apologize if I offended your sensibilities, Mrs. Conrad," Kate says coolly.

Our time with the Conrads continues in this vein. Becka spins fanciful tales of her very best friend, the dear departed, while Victor sits silently at her side, a stranger in his own house, and, apparently, his marriage. Detective Jerry stands off by the windows, jotting down notes in his ever present pad. He's letting us run the show while he watches and listens to the proceedings. He doesn't miss an inflection. Kate did her best to disguise her overwhelming contempt for the virtual couple and their ice palace of a home – she wasn't very successful – which leaves me in charge of navigating the frigid waters.

"Mrs. Conrad, Mr. Conrad, I believe we've taken up enough of your time this afternoon. Detective Maroney, do you have anything else you'd like to ask the Conrads?"

"No," he says, still writing. He avoids eye contact with Becka, who looks at him with an expression of dismay for the way he clashes with her home.

"I have one last question, if I may," says Kate. "Mrs. Conrad, knowing now how close you and Ms. Montgomery were and appreciating how helpful you've been in painting a more detailed picture of all that you shared, do you have any personal opinions as to the identity of the killer?" She didn't add the words 'you arrogant, preening bitch', though they were understood by everyone in the room and hung in the air like noxious fumes.

"Victor and I were with many of our social circle, and you, at the Audubon event on the night of the incident. I believe that is what's referred to as an alibi, Ms. Lindsey, for all of us. So, no, I really have no idea. I think Carla was robbed and killed by a stranger who envied the way she lived, the way we all live, and the more time your merry little band wastes investigating people like us, the more time the real killer has to disappear into the sewers, only to reappear at Nan's or Trisha's or here. And I'm sure that would make you very happy, wouldn't it, Ms. Lindsey?" Her voice never waivers, her expression never changes.

There's no discernible emotion in this woman at all, other than a general, weary disdain.

"No, Mrs. Conrad, were anything to happen to Mrs. Gibson, I wouldn't be happy at all. I'll show myself out. Able, Jerry, I'll wait for you downstairs." As she stands, Kate turns and smooths the fabric on the couch where she's been sitting and makes a show of repositioning the pillows just so. She moves across the room like a queen, pauses in front of the foyer table, looks down at it's carefully arranged objets, reaches over to the small, skeletal Giacometti-like sculpted figure, turns it about 30° and slides it back one inch. "That's better," she says to no one in particular.

As Kate leaves the room, Mrs. Conrad says, in a voice barely masking her annoyance, "I don't think your Ms. Lindsey cares for us, Able. Now, if you'll excuse us, Victor and I do have another engagement."

Victor still hasn't responded in any way. He sits on the couch, hidden beneath the shining bright layers of fame, fortune and success so carefully earned by him and carefully polished by his wife. He is a man with everything who wants for nothing. He is powerful, envied and utterly sad.

I offer him my hand. "Victor, thank you for your time. You know, I also knew Carla... well," I say, "It's a great loss." Victor's eyes meet mine.

Detective Jerry extends his hand as well. "If you think of anything, anything at all, please call anytime." He hands him his card, which Becka intercepts.

"Yes, certainly," he says quietly.

"Thank you, gentlemen. We will." she says, "Now, if you don't mind..."

"Of course, Mrs. Conrad, Mr. Conrad," says Detective Jerry. I bow my head slightly. It seems appropriate.

Becka escorts us to the door. As she passes the foyer table, her hand floats out and slides the small sculpted figure back into its original position. She doesn't stop, she doesn't look.

She doesn't have to.

35. Amateurs Steal, Professionals Borrow

Something looks familiar.

Sidney stands in the middle of her loft. She's wearing a *Guns and Roses* T-shirt and roomy striped boxer shorts, the left-behind souvenirs of a former boyfriend. Hated him, loved the boxers. As she sips her coffee, black and strong, she studies the paintings lined up against the wall – a massive Jackson Pollock drip extravaganza, a delicate Degas ballet study, a whimsical Chagall dream, a frightening Francis Bacon nightmare. And on and on, fifteen in all. Each one a marked contrast to the one before. Each one immensely valuable in its own right. Each one painted by Sidney and two of them not yet dry.

Not forgeries exactly, since none of them were signed with legible signatures. They were imitations – "in the style of...". Carla called them "custom work". It was their own little cottage industry. One they jokingly referred to as *Montgomery Masterpieces*.

It had started with a Winslow Homer river scene – a beautiful little oil in the Philadelphia Museum. Sidney had gone to the museum with her mother, as they often did on Saturday mornings. That was their special place. Something they'd shared for as long as Sidney could remember. She idolized her mother growing up. Her beauty, her grace, her intelligence. Cassandra seemed to know everything about everything. Art, though, was her special field of interest and when it became apparent that Sidney had a talent and a true curiosity, Cassandra was thrilled to share her own enthusiasm and nurture her daughter's gifts.

Unfortunately, her nurturing could often cross over into harsh criticism and cruel superiority. She could praise her daughter's intuitive understanding of a piece with words bordering on poetry, then, in an instant, castigate her for being presumptuous and pretentious – a "nefarious sycophant." Sidney had to look that one up and was stunned at the definition.

She didn't understand her mother's duality. It scared and confused her. She did, however, notice it was always worse in the afternoon, after her mother enjoyed her cocktails.

She also noticed, when she was around 12 or 13 years old, that something seemed to have happened between her mother and father and her older sister, Carla, whom she adored. Carla, the perfect sister, who sailed through Vassar and Yale, and breezed through Oxford, was suddenly not around very much and not mentioned very often. With that icy reserve perfected by old school WASPs, her mother responded to questions about Carla with, "Your sister is growing up, dear. She has her own life now." Case closed.

When Sidney asked Carla what had happened, Carla replied, "This doesn't concern you, Sid. And don't let it. Don't get in the middle of something you can't possibly understand."

For the rest of her teen years, whenever the sisters would see each other, Sidney felt Carla's eyes examining her, as if looking for signs of damage. She took a profound interest in Sidney's art and was her biggest champion. She also asked if mother was drinking any more or less than usual, if father was behaving, whatever that meant, and if Thorne seemed to be all right.

Carla was always home for the holidays and Sidney looked forward to these visits. There would be stolen moments when the two would go off together and her glamorous, nearly famous sister would regale her with stories of life in New York City. Sidney loved these stories. She thought she had the most amazing sister imaginable and hoped they would always be special to one another.

The rest of the holiday visits would play out with unsettling performances of masked emotions. Their father would desperately try to engage Carla's attention, but to no avail. Their mother and Carla would square off in an eerily well-mannered game of mental chess, though what the prize was, Sidney was hard pressed to discern.

And little brother Thorne, so pretty, so fine, would be alternately ridiculed by his father and smothered with affection by his mother, signs of his later dissolute confusion already mockingly evident in the calligraphic lines of worry and distrust that flew across his face with such alarming speed.

Sidney watched these goings on, the least conspicuous participant in the Chase Montgomery family drama, at least for now. She did what inconspicuous middle children do. She maintained peace. She filled gaps. She made everything all right.

She protected her little brother and calmed her father, entertained her mother and played handmaiden to her sister. It was an exhausting role, but one she preferred to the alternatives.

When Sidney was around 18, she realized she'd become something of an innocent pawn in her mother's and sister's ongoing competition. They had each been observing Sidney's growing artistic gifts with a combination of pride and fascination. Both women wanted to guide her course. Both wanted to be her emotional and intellectual benefactor. The attention was overwhelming. So was the stress.

Carla took to sending her truckloads of books she thought Sidney should be reading. Biographies and text books, collections of theoretical essays and academic dissertations on <u>The Politics of Art</u>. She wrote letters to Sidney expounding the revolutionary in art, *women's role in art, art as commerce, the marketing of genius. The seeds of some of Carla's best writing were sewn in these letters to her sister.*

Cassandra, in her uniquely schizophrenic fashion, continued to tutor and challenge Sidney with extemporaneous dinner lectures and their, by now, mandatory Saturday morning museum outings. It was on one of these Saturdays that Cassandra was extolling the genius of Winslow Homer; the fluidity of his technique, the graphic strength of his composition. She singled out a comparatively small, seemingly unobtrusive river scene and, through the elegant sensitivity of her insight and the orchestral power of her vocabulary, she had managed to convince Sidney that this was the best painting ever created, period, the end. Mona who? Whistler's what? Both, overproduced and overstated.

"If I were a thief," Cassandra said to her daughter, in a playfully wicked tone, "I would spirit this little gem out of the museum and hang it in our garden room, where I could look on it every morning and live a perfectly blissful existence." They laughed together as they often still did before the truth changed everything.

That Christmas, as a surprise for her mother, Sidney painted a copy of the Homer. She worked very hard on it and even surprised herself with how well it turned out. When Cassandra unwrapped her special gift on Christmas morning, Sidney watched with nervous anticipation as her mother's expression changed from shock to confusion to realization to amazement.

Carla, by now a celebrated critic, was present to witness her mother's reaction to the gift. "Mother?" she asked, "What is it?"

Cassandra looked up at Sidney with unbounded pride, then turned the painting toward Carla and said, "You tell me."

"Homer?" she said incredulously, "It's beautiful. But," turning to her baby sister, "Sid, how did you," then noticing the look her mother and sister shared, "What am I missing here?"

"Your genius of a sister has perfectly recreated a Winslow Homer and she did it for her mother." Cassandra glanced at Carla with an odd expression of victory. "Sidney, I'm speechless. This is the most wonderful present I've ever received."

Sidney was excited that her mother was so pleased, but strangely ill at ease as she watched Carla and Cassandra analyzing the implications of her growing talents.

The following year, when Sidney went on to college at the Tyler School of Art, then one of the best painting schools in the country, she looked forward to getting a break from the overwhelming influences of her mother and sister. That was a naive hope at best. Now they were even more interested in augmenting her good-enough-for-everyone-else-but-not-good-enough-for-our-Sidney education.

Her teachers and fellow students were not about to allow Sidney to forget her lineage, either. Her achievements and prodigious talents were revered and reviled in equal measure, for as undeniable as her talent was, the same could be said of her name.

Cassandra had decided that Sidney would be the next great woman painter. She was thrilled at the prospect and horribly jealous at the same time. But what an achievement for the family!

Carla was also becoming more and more certain of her sister's future importance in the art world; but based on her own experiences and observations, she did not delude herself into thinking that talent alone would be enough. Not for a woman, even if her family name was Chase Montgomery. She herself had had to work like ten men to achieve her current status – naturally, she made it all look effortless; in truth, it was anything but – and she was never allowed to forget her lineage, even though she'd been completely cut off financially since school and had cut her name in half at the same time, removing the connection to her mother. So, instead, she used it like a weapon. She hurled her stature in their faces. And she found that men were excited by it. Women, on the other hand, hated her for it. Carla hadn't counted on that. She assumed that all women would stand behind the success of one of their own. She thought they would cheer her on – good show Carla! – but it didn't work that way, in her career or in her social life.

Carla didn't think Sidney was tough enough to do what was necessary to build her career. She wanted to help her succeed, but she knew that an art critic supporting a new talent who happened to be her baby sister would only be viewed as rank nepotism, thereby making Sid an easy target. Her career would be destroyed before it was even begun. No, Carla knew that to help her sister she had to distance herself professionally. She'd even go further. She would take the public stance that women on the whole do not belong in the arts, that they don't have what it takes. She would use everything that had been used against her and repackage those hateful words as her own astute observations on women, thereby setting a stage on which Sidney could shine. Other critics would set her up as an example to disprove Carla's theories. Galleries would court her to benefit from the publicity generated by famously opposite sisters.

The plan moved forward and Sid watched with fascination as her beloved sister acted the role of worst enemy. Sometimes the cruel remarks and public coldness were difficult to bear – Carla could be very convincing – but late at night on the telephone, they would giggle like schoolgirls and chart the development of Sidney's reputation and career.

Of course, it takes time to build a legend. And in the meantime, Sidney needed to eat. She, like her sister, had been cut off financially as soon as her schooling was completed, in spite of her mother's, shall we say, 'challenging' support. Carla helped out, but she was still perfecting her own persona and that took money. Besides, Sid wanted to earn her own keep, be independent, and make a living from her art.

Enter Eleanor Vesprey, interior decorator to the rich and richer. Carla was introduced to Eleanor at a cocktail party given by their mutual friend, Shawn Patrik. Shawn introduced her by her pet name, Lamb. 'Such an annoying child-like name,' thought Carla. "I dislike her already.' But much to her surprise and everyone else's, the ladies became fast friends, seeing in each other an outsider very much on the inside. As the evening wore on, as their conversation continued, as one cocktail became two, then three, then four, the need to impress and be impressed relaxed into a comfortable rapport, rich in a healthy disrespect for practically everything.

Eleanor was entertaining Carla and Shawn with the saga of one of her current clients. Lots of gestures. Lots of drama.

"So the wife – we shall call her La Femme Quatre, *because she is, after all, the fourth wife – has decided she would like her portrait to hang above the mantle in the formal living room, and she would like said portrait to be painted by Botticelli – Botticelli, mind you! – and would I take care of arranging it. I informed the stupid little thing that Botticelli was, in fact, dead, and therefore, the commission would be difficult. Well, do you know that she simply would not accept that as an excuse. Dead or alive, Botticelli must paint her portrait!* The Birth of Venus, *apparently inspired her to become a blonde and, of course, her life was never the same, as a result. When presented with such a moving account of someone's personal connection to great art, I did what any self-respecting engineer of the inflated image would do."*

"What?" asked Shawn and Carla in unison.

"I said, 'Not to worry, my darling angel, Lamb will take care of everything.'"

"And how do you propose to do that?" asked Shawn.

"I have no idea," she sipped her champagne, "but it won't be inexpensive."

"If I could interject," said Carla.

"Please," said Eleanor.

"As it happens, I know of someone, a new and rising talent, who can mimic any style convincingly. Also, she has a gift for capturing a likeness. I'm sure, combining the two wouldn't be a problem."

"Marvelous!" exclaimed Eleanor.

"Why haven't I heard about this 'new and rising talent' before?" asked Shawn skeptically.

"As I said, she's new," said Carla.

"New or old, I don't really care, as long as she can do it," said Eleanor, "and if you say she can, my dear, then I'm sure she can. Of course I trust you implicitly."

"Lamb, you don't trust anyone," said Shawn.

"Her, Shawny, I trust her." Eleanor and Carla exchanged a knowing look. "We're the same, you and I."

"Yes, I think so."

"Shall I call you tomorrow to set this farce in motion?"

"Do. We can work out the details of...what is the client's name?"

"Stefani... with an 'i'."

"Perfect. We can work out the details of The Birth of Stefani with an 'i'. I, of course, will act as the artist's agent."

"Of course," said Eleanor. "And might we know the artist's name?"

"Not just yet," said Carla. "Might I know the budget for the piece?"

"Not just yet," said Eleanor. "Deal then?"

"Deal."

They clinked glasses as Shawn said, "Is this the beginning of some cabal? Some secret society? Have I opened the door to evil here in my own home?"

"It wouldn't be the first time, Sweetie," said Carla as the two ladies kissed him on opposite cheeks.

Thus began Montgomery Masterpieces.

"I do have one question though, if you don't mind?," asked Carla. "Lamb? What's that about? You don't seem like a Lamb to me."

Eleanor Vesprey smiled," Awful isn't it? But this crowd loves that nonsense. Darling, they could call me Buttercup if they wanted to. As long as they pay my prices, I don't really care."

"I've met my match, Shawn." Carla was enjoying herself. "Lamb, if I may, I think you and I are going to be very good friends."

"Get ready for the Apocalypse!" sighed Shawn.

After the success of the pseudo-Botticelli, Eleanor asked Carla if she thought Sidney – Carla had divulged her sister's identity to Eleanor in private on the condition that she tell no one, including Shawn – could recreate a Paul Klee on a larger scale for a Texas client, who had said, in her long, languorous Texas drawl that made every sentence sound like a question, "It was a wedding present from one of my husband's business partners. It's pretty and all, but it's so darn small. Do you think we could bump it up a little bit?"

Then came a false Seurat of a Virginia equestrian's prized estate view, followed by a variation on a New York collector's favorite Clifford Still, but this one was for the Hamptons beach house so, "Could we lighten the palette just a touch?"

Sidney was appalled by the requests and repeatedly refused to be a part of such a disgrace, but Carla would calm her down, reminding her that she was perfecting her skills, that her anonymity was protected, and that she was making a very good living from their bizarre venture.

Eleanor Vesprey, for her part, was formulating the next logical step for their little enterprise – helping certain clients fill the gaps in their already impressive collections. Obviously, if one owns a Monet, a VanGogh and a Degas, no one's going to question the validity of the charming little Mary Cassatt-like pastel that looks so right in the powder room. Or, let's say a person owns three very beautiful Rothkos, but four would positively make the downstairs study...not a problem.

Eleanor very clearly explained to her clients that these were not forgeries. No laws were being broken. No claims were being made. These were decorations. Additions to an obvious esthetic equation. And what's more, they were, comparatively speaking, a bargain.

So clear in concept. So smooth in execution. And, oh so very lucrative. Eleanor handled the clients, Sidney handled the paintings and Carla handled Sidney. Simple as 1-2-3.

And that's how it had worked for the last few years. Sidney had a more than comfortable income, the source of which no one ever questioned. She was, after all, a Chase Montgomery. She could live quite well and, for the most part, concentrate on nurturing her own career which continued to develop as Carla said it would, fueled by the growing legend of the battling sisters.

Carla and Eleanor enjoyed their increased wealth but, more than that, revelled in their ability to manipulate that unique circle where high-end art and high society overlap. It was all a great joke to them. A mean-spirited joke. For Eleanor, it was a personal vendetta, mocking the kinds of people who had mocked her so long ago. For Carla it was more of an entertainment.

Sidney pretended not to notice. She'd never liked Eleanor, and adamantly refused to refer to her by her overly precious nickname, but as long as Carla was around, she never had to deal with her directly. And as for Carla herself? Sidney had started to see her as the ultimate chameleon. She was whatever you needed or wanted her to be -- as long as there was something in it for her. Was the world really this ugly and false or had they just made it this way?

Sidney finishes her coffee and puts out her cigarette in the cup. She sets the cup on the floor. She walks across the loft to the bathroom, removing her T-shirt, stepping out of her boxers. As she turns on the faucets and enters the shower, as she feels the gentle pin pricks of the warm water chip away at her pain, her loss, her shame, her guilt, Sidney lowers her head and says to herself, "No more."

36. A Clearing in the Distance

I think I see something.

"Obviously Lamb Vesprey is the L.V. in Carla's day-timer," says Kate to me and Detective Jerry as we walk down Fifth Avenue,"and Hugo said he was meeting with her at the gallery at 5:00. It's just 5:00 now. Shall we?"

We flag a cab and head down to Chelsea.

"Lamb," says Kate, shaking her head,"isn't that a ridiculous nickname?"

"I don't know Kitten," says I,"do you really think so?"

Kate sneers. The detective clears his throat."Play nice. We're making progress here, thanks to you two. I agree, L.V. is probably Ms. Vesprey. We're able to access the last five years of Carla's calendar and correspondence, and L.V. appears long before Leo Ventura was on the scene."

"Well, I'm sure she's involved somehow," says Kate.

"Based on what? You don't even know her," says I.

"Call it intuition. Women like that aren't casual friends. They don't have the time for it. And what about the news flash about both of them being self-made? Able, had you ever heard that before?"

"No. And I never would have guessed. Both of them use – or used their ancestry as a selling point. You know...I'm thinking...when I knew Carla, she was living really well."

"She made a good income," says Kate.

"Not that good. This was before the books and TV appearances and all that."

"So she lived beyond her means. That's hardly unique in New York. And I'm sure her gentlemen callers were generous, weren't they?" says Kate, batting her eyelashes.

"If they could afford to be... but it's still not enough. That would explain the wardrobe and maybe even the furniture, but that doesn't explain the art collection. I never thought about it because the family's loaded, and I figured she could buy whatever she wanted or just borrow from the family vault. But if she was cut off and living on a columnist's income... no way."

"So, what are you saying? You think she stole them?" asks Detective Jerry.

"That doesn't make sense. We aren't talking about one or two paintings here. More like ten or twelve. And they all appeared to be major. At least as I recall. But that was a long time ago and I was looking at other things."

"Spare me," says Kate.

"Detective, after we're done at Hugo's, could we go to Carla's apartment? I'd like to have a look at the art."

"Absolutely. You're the expert."

As the car pulls up in front of the gallery, we can see that Eleanor Vesprey is still inside talking with Hugo. We enter the gallery and Hugo waves us over.

"Here's the artist now. All three musketeers, in fact. Miss Vesprey and I were just discussing two of your pieces, Able."

"Yes and they're glorious!" says Eleanor, as she removes her half-glasses and holds them in her left hand, the better with which to gesticulate. "So powerful and yet so sensitive! So grand and yet so simple!"

"So dark and yet so light?" offers Kate.

"Exactly! How do you do. Eleanor Vesprey."

"Kate Lindsey, Miss Vesprey. It's a pleasure."

"Thank you. And you, sir, are Detective Maroney I believe?" she asks as she offers him her hand,"And the three of you are investigating Carla's murder. Such a tragedy, such a loss. Please tell me it's been solved."

"We're getting closer, Ma'am," said the detective. "If you wouldn't mind, when you and Mr. Swann are finished, I was wondering if we might ask you a few questions?"

"Of course, of course. Actually, we've just this minute concluded, haven't we Hugo? Am I forgetting anything?"

"Let me see. These pieces are on hold, this group we're shipping to the Raymonds' apartment –"

"But *not* before Wednesday."

"Yes, not before Wednesday. And these last four and Able's two pieces we're delivering to your office tomorrow before 5:00. That's it."

"Fabulous! Hugo, darling, what would I do without you? You're so fortunate, Mr. Ryder, to be working with our elegant Mr. Swann. Now, let me gather my things. Where shall we –"

"You can use my office if you'd like; more privacy. Tess is finishing up some filing. I'll ask her to help me out here with Miss Vesprey's pieces."

"Thank you, Mr. Swann," says Detective Jerry.

"Not a problem."

"We were friends, true friends, and I miss her dreadfully," Eleanor Vesprey begins to speak before the door to the office is closed. "I'm sure you've heard terrible things about Carla. That she was cold, calculating...indiscreet. Well, none of them knew her the way I did. We were alike, she and I. Misfits." She absentmindedly rotates a delicate gold bracelet around her pencil thin wrist. "You know they all resented her."

"*They* being?" asks Kate.

"Oh, everyone. The crowd."

"And aren't you one of that crowd?" asks Kate.

"Yes, but I also make my living from them. There's a difference. And that's what Carla and I shared. We were working girls in a sorority of pampered princesses. And they hated her for her brains, her beauty, her inborn style. Granted, she inherited them – you've met Cassandra – but she earned her fame and fortune, not to mention confidence, on her own. Any one of those women would just as soon see her dead as have their nails done. She got in their way and made them look bad by comparison."

"I'm sure she was remarkable, Miss Vesprey, but you must admit, she did invite enmity if only by stealing so many husbands," says Kate.

"It's not stealing, Ms. Lindsey, if it's given to you. Men loved Carla and she returned the favor."

"Miss Vesprey,"says Detective Jerry, "in reading through Ms. Montgomery's journals we often come across the initials L.V..."

Ms. Vesprey smiles,"Yes, that would be me. My social friends know me as Lamb," she turns to look at Kate, "a ludicrous name for a grown woman, don't you agree? But they seem to like it. Part of the charade." Kate visibly winces, hearing Ms. Vesprey pronounce the word *sha-**rod***.

Ms. Vesprey redirects her comments to the detective,"At any rate, Carla thought it was condescending and instead chose to call me L.V. She thought it sounded strong and direct, two words she often used to describe me."

She removes a handkerchief from her handbag and dabs at the corners of her eyes.

"Miss Vesprey," continues Detective Jerry, "there seem to be many appointments in which the two of you would meet at galleries or museums."

"Yes, I would often consult with Carla regarding my clients' art."

"In regard to..."

"In regard to value, history, appropriate presentation, authenticity. Also acquisitions. I trusted her completely."

Conversation is interrupted by the ringing of Detective Jerry's cell phone."Yes... o.k., I'll be there in ten."

"What's up?" I ask.

"Something back at the station. Miss Vesprey, thank you for taking the time to speak with us this evening. You've been very helpful. May I call you if we have any additional questions about Ms. Montgomery?"

"Please. Let me give you my card."

Goodbyes are exchanged. Eleanor Vesprey wraps herself in Chanel and exits the gallery, after blowing a poised two finger kiss to Hugo and Tess. "Kisses!" she calls out lightly, and then she's gone.

While the detective sends a quick text, Kate says to me,"You were awfully quiet."

"I was enjoying the performance."

"Sincere or insincere?"

"Fifty-fifty. Eleanor Vesprey's not that soft. Something doesn't ring true."

The detective puts the phone back in his coat pocket. "I've cleared access for you at the Montgomery apartment, if you still want to check out the paintings tonight. I've got to get back. It seems I was sent a special delivery package – a manuscript of Carla Montgomery's unpublished autobiography."

37. Stranger in a Strange Land

Next?

Eleanor Vesprey sits in the back of the cab, fingering a charm on her bracelet. It's a miniature Baroque picture frame – a gift from Carla.

She settles back and tries to put it all out of her mind. As the cab continues downtown, through Chelsea, through the Village, she looks out the window into the early evening, watching the city roll by. That's how it always felt to her, when riding in a cab – that you were stationary and the panorama of New York was moving past you, just out of reach. Not that you wanted to touch it. Think what you might catch.

But in the relative safety of the backseat, with windows up and locks secured, she has to admit there's a dangerous glamour to this part of town, a seedy allure to the shadows and the angles and all of those people. Downtown city people with their swagger and blunt style – part warrior, part fashion model – demanding attention and refusing to acknowledge any.

How often had Carla told Eleanor about her downtown escapades? She'd loved it here. "What could be more fun," she'd say after an elegant Sutton Place cocktail party, "than trolling the college bars near NYU looking for the cutest sophomore, then teaching him a thing or two in the nearest darkened doorway? I'll call you tomorrow and let you know if I majored in French or minored in Greek."

Eleanor smiled and shook her head at the memory. Carla loved to shock – the sophomores just as much as the ambassadors, and the leather boys just as much as the society girls. Eleanor lived vicariously through her daring friend. That was one of the things she missed most. In truth, she'd continued with the art business only to have a reason, an excuse, to be in Carla's life on an almost daily basis. She had seen, often enough, how easily bored Carla could become and how effortlessly she could dismiss people, even joking about it. "It's a family trait, L.V.," she'd say. "The Chase Montgomerys aren't nice, because we don't have to be."

But she was nice, or could be. She was sweet even. I understood her the way no one else did. She didn't have to shock me or entertain me. She didn't have to pretend to be anything at all. She was Carla. Just Carla.

The cab pulls up in front of a dark grey building – at one time, a factory of some sort and probably not dark grey – on lower Broadway. Most of the elegant architectural details of the turn-of-the-last-century structure had been obscured by years of exposure to the elements, both natural and man-made. It had been beautiful once. Impressive. But beauty doesn't last, and impressions change.

Eleanor pays the driver and gets out of the cab. She stands on the sidewalk at odds with her surroundings, an inappropriate addition to the downtown urban landscape. She feels conspicuous. She is.

As she checks for her handbag, making sure it's still attached to her arm, Eleanor Vesprey sets her jaw, arches her brow, smooths her hair, and enters the building.

"This should be interesting," she says to herself.

38. Window Shopping

Trying on the merch.

Quality time. Dusk in the city. Kate and I decide to walk to Carla Montgomery's apartment from Hugo's gallery, rather than take a cab. Chelsea to the Upper East Side. A chance to play catch up, to window shop and possibly stop for a cocktail.

"This is what I miss most, living in the country. I love a long walk in New York."

"Urban aerobics and all the visual stimuli you could ever need."

"That's the truth. Tell me, how do you walk in those things?" Kate was still wearing 4 inches of towering pain.

"These old things? They're nothing. Any anguish is offset by how good my calves look."

"You know, Kitten, you do look good. Really good. I think this investigator lifestyle agrees with you."

"Thank you, it does, and what's with this 'Kitten' business?"

"Just trying it on for size. I never gave you a nickname before. How do you like it?"

"Touching. Like a cold sore. Keep at it and I'll think up something equally adorable for you."

"Okay, I'll behave. But you *are* challenged by this investigation, aren't you? Can't say I never showed you an interesting time."

"I haven't been able to say that since you positioned me directly behind the nude model in freshman drawing class. What was his name? Babycakes?"

"That's what we called him. See, another adorable nick-name."

"In his case, it was very appropriate, as I recall."

We slow down at Saks, checking out the merchandise on display in the windows.

"It's like an oddly perfect world in there, isn't it?" says Kate, "Perfect clothes, perfect hair, perfect rooms all perfectly appointed."

"Perfect little cracks where everything is pieced together."

"Obvious analogy noted."

We link arms as we continue north on Fifth past St. Patrick's.

"Aren't you glad we're us, Able?"

"Every waking minute."

"No, seriously. I mean, you and I do all right, much better than all right, truth be told, but you always wonder if it's enough. At least I do. What if I had more money? What if I were beautiful? What if I was famous?"

"You make good money, you are beautiful, and you're known and respected in your field."

"Yes, but – and thanks for the 'beautiful' thing – but I mean big money, mega-money, and drop-dead gorgeous and *People* magazine famous."

"I'm listening."

"So here we've been meeting all of these people who have the whole deal and look at them. Miserable. Except for my new best friend Nan, of course, but I think she's probably the exception that proves the rule."

"Check. And check. So, here's to the wonder that is us."

"Sounds like a toast without a cocktail. And you know what that's like –"

"A D-List celebrity without a reality show?"

"Precisely. Now let's see, what are we near...I know. *Endive*'s just a few blocks. It's the place to be this month. I'm thinking... martinis!"

"I'm thinking... yes!"

39. Every Picture Tells a Story

The Buddy system.

When we enter the crowded restaurant, Kate grabs my hand and says, "You're out of practice. Let me lead."

She plows through the throng and captures two bar stools just this second being vacated by two young secretaries hoping against hope that they appear to be worldly, sophisticated girls-about-town.

"Success!"

"When it comes to the prospect of comfort and cocktails, you're like a heat-seeking missile."

"Thank you for noticing."

She flags down the bartender and orders. "The gentleman will have a vodka martini, straight up with olives. And in honor of my new best friend, make mine a Gibson."

We survey the room while we wait for our drinks to arrive.

"Nice," says I.

"It is, isn't it? And do you know who designed it? Shawn Patrik."

"Small world."

"And getting smaller. He just walked in – with Victor Conrad."

Victor is laughing at something Shawn is whispering. He's aloof to the surroundings, pretending not to be noticed. Shawn, on the other hand, nods to this one, winks at that one, waves, smiles, works the crowd from the front door. When he catches sight of us at the bar, he heads straight for us, bringing a reluctant Victor Conrad with him.

"Kevin," Shawn says to the bartender, "Whatever they're having, put it on my tab."

"Thank you Shawn. That's very nice. I'd like you to meet..."

"Kate Lindsey. Your partner in crime solving," Shawn takes Kate's hand and holds it gently,"Mrs. Gibson was very taken with you. I've already had a complete description. She likes your style."

"Oh my. I'm trying hard to look blasé," turning toward me, "It's not working, is it?"

"Afraid not."

"If it makes you feel more comfortable, Ms. Lindsey, I heard a very different description from Victor's wife."

"I'm sure you did," says Kate, twirling the onion in her drink.

"I should apologize for Becka," says Victor, "My wife can be...difficult."

"And Iceland can be chilly," counters Shawn. "Victor has a way of understating the obvious, don't you, V?" He punches Victor lightly in the arm. Victor looks charmingly chagrined.

Kate is struck by how attractive the two men are. She's seen Shawn often enough, but had never been introduced. Known for his dazzle, he doesn't disappoint. Victor, however, is a revelation. They'd just met him a few hours ago and yes, he was handsome; but this Victor, the one standing before her now, is much more at ease, much more relaxed than he'd been in his own home in the company of his own wife. This Victor looks like the confident power player he's said to be. Yes, she thought, Victor and Shawn are an impressive couple of gentlemen – one dark and rugged, one blond and elegant; both fit and trim and playful. Like former frat boys. Like crew mates. Like... 'Oh,' she stops mid-thought, 'I think I get it now.'

She tunes back in as Shawn is saying, "We all appreciate so much what you and Ms. Lindsey are doing. Well, I do anyway. And I know that you'll unravel this mystery soon. Again, if there's any way I can help, please let me know. Now, if you'll excuse us, I think our table's ready. Anything you want, it's on me."

Goodbyes are exchanged and the two men move through the room to their awaiting table, Shawn's hand on Victor's shoulder, guiding him along.

"Shawn's a good guy," I say as I motion to the bartender. "Two more of the same, Kevin. Thanks."

"Victor Conrad would agree with you," says Kate, watching as they get situated at their table.

"Apparently, they're good friends. Just came from their weekly handball date."

"No doubt."

"Do I detect a note of sarcasm?"

"Maybe just a tad."

"So? What is it?"

"Victor and Shawn. They're an item."

"You've gotta be kidding."

"I'm a single city woman of a certain age. Believe me, I know the signs."

"But Victor's..."

"What? Married? That doesn't mean anything."

"How about the affair with Carla?"

Kate thinks for a long minute, twirling the stem of her glass in her hand. "How do we know there was an affair? Maybe she was a go-between for her best friend and this new guy in town...or maybe she did have an affair with Victor, a brief one, but it didn't work out because, well, she could tell, and Carla, being Carla, was cool with that, so she played matchmaker with him and Shawn, who already knew him since he was working on the Conrad's apartment and was attracted to him, which is certainly understandable. And there was definitely no palpable evidence of a physical attraction between Mr. and Mrs. Conrad when we saw them, was there? So, if he was already leaning that way, Victor I mean, it makes perfect sense he would lean right into Shawn, who has to be one of the best looking men I've ever seen in my life!"

"You're so clever, you are."

"I know."

"Must be exhausting."

"Truly."

I look over toward Shawn's and Victor's table and notice how they lean into each other as they speak, how they never lose eye contact, how warm their facial expressions are.

"Assuming you're right..."

"Which I am."

"What does that mean in relation to Carla?"

"Maybe nothing. Maybe everything. Maybe she really was attracted to Victor and was disappointed once too often. It's not easy always seeing the great guys go off into the sunset arm in arm."

"Voice of experience?"

"Maybe just a little. Be that as it may, maybe she threatened to expose Victor and he wasn't ready to deal with it. He went to reason with her, and things got out of hand."

"Or maybe Shawn wanted to protect Victor, he went to do the reasoning, and things got out of hand."

We both squint off into the distance as Kate says, "The plot thickens!"

"You had to say it, didn't you?"

"You're just mad you didn't say it first"

We finish our second round in record time and take one last look at the table across the room.

"The apartment?"Kate suggests.

"The apartment." I reply.

40. Architecture Redigested

It's all in the details.

The door to Carla Montgomery's apartment is sealed with yellow tape marked CRIME SCENE DO NOT CROSS. A uniformed police officer stands guard. After the requisite identification process, we're issued latex gloves, told not to move anything, and, finally, allowed entry. The officer remains at his post.

As Kate stands in the middle of the living room doing a slow 360° turn, taking it all in, I move directly to a large canvas hanging in the entry.

"This is really something," says Kate, "Different. Able, I think Carla was as big a collector of everything as you are."

"Yes, but at a different price point. It's still pretty much as it was years ago. Just...more so. Say what you want, she had a great eye."

Kate doesn't respond.

"What, no witty comeback? No, 'What was wrong with the other one?'"

"Too easy," she pauses. "I hate to admit it but..."

"But, you're beginning to like Carla aren't you?"

"I wouldn't go that far, but I'm beginning to understand her better," she walks around the living room, eyes constantly moving, not missing a thing. "All the residences we've seen lately are beautiful. It's a given. Even the Conrad's ice palace. But this...I don't know...it's a real work of art. This isn't the home of a bad person. This is the home of a...a rigorously smart, extremely sensitive, inherently unique artist. I happen to know somebody else who fits that description, so I know what I'm talking about here."

"And you get all of that just by walking into the room?"

"And by the way people speak about her. People who think they knew her, then realize as they're talking, that they didn't really. I see a woman who made herself tough to survive and who made herself desirable to succeed. I see a woman who had points to prove and scores to settle. I see a woman who was disappointed in the limitations of others, and the limitations they tried to impose on her. I see a woman who wanted love desperately, but purposely sabotaged her own chances with inappropriate choices. I see a woman too close to me for comfort."

"You see a lot," I say softly.

"I've got a great eye." She assumes an ironic expression; an arched brow, a knowing smile. Seeking out a comfortable place to stand, where she'll also be out of harm's way, Kate asks, "So, what were you looking at in the entry hall?"

"Looks like a Barnett Newman."

Kate turns to look back at the very large canvas. All she sees is a giant blue rectangle with two vertical white lines. She has a scarf just like it at home.

"But you're not sure?"

"I'm reserving judgement. Let's do an overall inventory, shall we?"

Kate leaned against the mantle piece as I begin a tour through the paintings on display in the living room. "Here we have what appears to be a Whistler. One of the Thames river studies. Beautiful variations of grey, wonderful design. Impressionist, almost abstract. Evocative."

"Lonely."

"You think?"

"Maybe melancholy is a better word."

"Definitely. You know, I don't like Whistler's people, including his mother, but he paints a great mood...the problem is...this mood is painted too well," I get up close to the canvas and look at the surface from the side, "He had a real bravura brush stroke, and these lack his confidence. They make the whole thing too pretty. More of an ideal, rather than an impression...it's a fake."

I turn to the right and step up to the painting hanging beside the Not-a-Whistler.

"Franz Kline. Interesting juxtaposition. Similar in its structure and economy but so different in its impact. The Whistler's pensive whereas this is..."

"Angry? Aggressive? Psychotic?"

"Not a fan of Mr. Kline?"

"Not on a daily basis."

"Well, whoever really painted this was a big fan."

"So, this isn't real either? How can you tell?"

"It's got the power...but none of the sadness."

Kate looks at me as if she's trying to decide whether *I'm* the real thing or a fake Able spouting pompous artspeak. "Sadness? It's a bunch of big, nasty slashes across an empty background."

"See? We agree. In a real Kline those slashes would be complex gestures of emotion. Like music. Like Miles Davis. Here, all we get is random noise."

"Are you making this up as you go along? Because that's very good. What say we turn down the volume and go onto the next one. This is like a private course in Art Appreciation. Professor...if you please."

Completing the grouping on this wall is a voluptuous, graphic composition of shapes in deep, dark, pulsing colors. Sensual, demanding, in your face. Georgia O'Keefe.

"Whistler, Kline, O'Keefe. An unexpected combination." I study this third piece as closely as I had the other two. "This is one of the Jack-in-the-Pulpit paintings, part of an endless parade of O'Keefe flowers, which are all about sex, as we know."

"I thought she said they weren't."

"She lied. Just look at it. Georgia was no shrinking violet. She knew how to be controversial. Some of her flowers, like the chrysanthemums and roses, are pretty, unfolding, waiting to be plucked. But the Jack-in-the-Pulpit is the hard-core master in her garden. Overripe and inescapable."

"My, my," says Kate, exaggeratedly fanning herself. "So, this one's the real deal?"

"No, but it's a very faithful copy of the real deal. Just smaller. I saw the original last month at an O'Keefe exhibit in Washington – the Phillips Collection."

I turn toward Kate,"Three for three. What do you make of that?"

"She didn't like to pay retail?"

I wince.

"Seriously," she continues. "You know they're fake because you came in here looking for them to be fake. Also, you're brilliant, and you know what to look for. But, to the untrained eye, of which I have two, I see paintings that look important and vaguely recognizable; and since they belong to Carla Montgomery, I figure they must be the genuine article and therefore, I'm impressed, which I believe is the point."

"Okay, but why so many and where did they come from? I can't think it would have been easy for someone as recognizable in the art world as Carla was, to buy or commission copies of this caliber."

"Maybe she had something on the artists who did these? Or maybe it's a whole underground fraud ring that she got wind of somehow and threatened to expose? Able? You just got that light-bulb-over-the-head look. What is it?"

"Maybe it was her ring. What do you think of that? Carla had a lot of disdain for museum-goers and art buyers in general. She didn't think any of them knew what they were looking at without being given a guide book, preferably the Cliff Note version."

"So she puts fake paintings on the market that she praises as real and then has a private chuckle at the expense of her well-to-do stooges. Clever idea. But where do the artists come from?"

"Any art school. Any struggling artist who can't make ends meet. Some people have a real gift for mimicry, for faking several different techniques. Wait! Is my light bulb showing again?"

"Maybe just a little."

"When we spoke with Leo Ventura, he told us how Carla was the best teacher he ever had, how she had him doing copies of a variety of realist styles to help him establish a base for his abstract work. And there was a very convincing Matisse on his work table, in progress. Maybe it's time to pay another visit to Leo."

41. Knock Knock

Who's there?

"His phone's still busy, so he must be home." We're downtown, in Leo Ventura's building, riding the elevator to his floor.

"But isn't this illegal, just showing up unannounced? Don't we need a search warrant or something?"

"We're not real police, remember? This is simply an impromptu social visit. One artist dropping in on another. That's all."

When we reach his floor, we see that the door to Leo's loft space is already open. We hear a woman's voice -- frantic, emotional, vaguely recognizable.

"Miss Vesprey?"

Eleanor Vesprey turns to see us standing in the doorway. She's holding her phone with a visibly shaking hand. Her face is pale, her expression, stricken.

"Oh, Mr. Ryder, Ms. Lindsey, I..." her mouth moves, but no words come out. The phone slips out of her hand as her knees begin to buckle. I grab her before she hits the floor and steer her into a nearby chair...she looks small, breakable and completely out of place, a waif in borrowed finery, a stick figure in fancy dress.

Kate picks up the phone, checking to see that the line is, in fact, dead and places it on the desk next to which Miss Vesprey had been standing.

"Eleanor," I say in a soothing tone as I kneel by her side, "what's happened? Where's Leo?"

Her head leaned against the back of the chair at an awkward angle, eyes closed. She took a long, shuddering breath before attempting to speak.

"The bedroom," she sighs. "He's in the bedroom. I don't know what happened." As she reaches toward her face, smoothing her forehead with the palm of her left hand,

I see the blood for the first time, dripping down her arm from her fingertips. I look over to Kate, who nods in recognition.

"I'll call the police," she says.

"They've been notified," says Eleanor, trying to sound competent and controlled, looking anything but.

"Kate, why don't you stay with Miss Vesprey, while I have a look in the other room."

I head cautiously toward the bedroom door, my heart is beating fast, too fast. Everything seems heightened. This is a moment you can't prepare for. This is a scene from a movie, not real life.

But it is real life and, unbelievably, I find myself looking through a doorway at a butchered corpse. It's Leo, or was, lying in a spreading pool of his own blood. He'd been stabbed repeatedly. He'd fought, apparently. The room was upended, everything in disarray.

42. The Same...but Different

Surprise!

Sidney finds herself in a much better mood. She'd taken herself to the movies, her favorite escape from life. Ever since she was a teen, Sid loved nothing more than buying one ticket, a large popcorn – hold the butter – and a ridiculously oversized Diet Coke, then sliding down in an aisle seat and waiting for the dark. She didn't have to pretend here. Those people on the screen were pretending for her.

She especially loved the old films from the '30s to the '50s. The black-and-white photography, the deep shadows and beautiful lighting, the mannered acting, the stylized details – all such a contrast to the way she lived. This evening, she had gone to the *Angelica* to see a revival of an old Kirk Douglas/Lana Turner movie, *The Bad and the Beautiful*. 'Okay,' she thought. 'Maybe this isn't so different after all. But at least it's happening to them and not me.'

For two hours, she was completely immersed in the story going on in front of her. In the past she would have phoned Carla as soon as she got home to talk about the film, reenacting favorite scenes, describing the clothes and the music...but that was before. As the credits rolled, Sid grabbed up her trash and headed for the exit. 'Carla would have loved this,' she said to herself.

Then she opened the door and stepped back into reality.

This reality wasn't half bad. It was close to midnight and stores were open, lights were blazing, people were hanging out, life was happening. This was the color and fabric of real life being lived by real people. People who worked hard and played rarely, people who found hope in a lotto ticket and love in a stolen glance. She was more like them than the family she'd been born into...or was she? Ah, the romance of struggle and strife when you don't have to experience it firsthand. Sidney took her time walking home, enjoying the city and all of its sights.

She arrives back at the loft around 12:30. As she enters the space, she hears a low, familiar voice.

"Hello, you."

Sidney jumps back, dropping her keys and the tulips she'd just gotten from the corner grocer.

"Thorne! Jesus, you scared the hell out of me!" He steps out of the shadows in a cloud of cigarette smoke. "Gotcha," he says, dryly.

"Not funny, Thorne," Sidney circles the loft with nervous energy, turning on lights as she goes. "What are you doing here?" She bends to pick up her scattered tulips, heart still pounding with an after-hours club beat.

"I needed a break from the homestead and thought I'd come see my favorite sister."

"Your only sister."

"My living sister."

"It's after midnight."

"So, call a cop." He takes a long drag off his cigarette, "I don't think you're happy to see me."

"What do you want, Thorne? And where have you been? Were you in a fight or something? You look like hell!"

He steps over to the artfully rusted construction dolly that acts as Sidney's coffee table and flicks his cigarette into a half-filled coffee cup. "Nevermind. Can't a guy just visit his sister?" He flops down onto the ornate Victorian fainting couch, which had been upholstered in a hot pink and red Marimekko print. "Nice place, by the way. A little bohemian for my taste, but there you are."

Sidney takes the tulips to the kitchen counter where she proceeds to arrange them in a favorite stoneware pitcher.

"I've been here for quite a while," Thorne continues. "Gave myself a tour. Knew you wouldn't mind. It appears you've been busy," he pauses, "I especially like the Francis Bacon."

Sidney stops what she's doing and looks at her brother.

"The Pollock's good, too," he continues, "but the Degas...I don't know. I don't think you have the sensitivity for Degas. Nothing personal, you understand. It's a family trait." He pulls out another cigarette and lights it, inhaling dramatically for effect. "Speaking of mother...she sends her love."

"What's this about, Thorne?"

"Family pride, I think. Mother wants your little forgery side line to end. She thinks it makes a mockery of your talent – your gift, as she likes to call it. I'm here strictly as the messenger."

"Mother's little toady."

"It's a living."

Sidney taps her fingers along the edge of the soapstone counter. "How long has she known, do you suppose?"

"Since time began. Mother knows all, haven't you realized that yet? Apparently Carla told her about it just after you started. She thought mother would be entertained by the concept and appreciative of the way she was helping her little sister make ends meet – wrong on both accounts. Mother thought Carla was blaspheming in the church of high art and that you were ruining any chance for a serious career."

"Neither of them ever said anything to me...when do they stop deciding how everything works, what everyone should do, even from the grave?" Sidney shakes her head slowly from side to side, as if to say,' No. No. No.' "Do you want to know something? I don't want to be an artist." She stops short, letting the statement reverberate. "There, I've said it out loud. I don't want to be an artist anymore."

"Butcha-are, Sid."

"No, I'm a mockery, like mother said." Her teeth are grinding. A cynical smile appears on her lips. "When you report back to mother, you can tell her she's won again. I'd already decided that I was done with the fakes, and now, thanks to your visit, I've decided I'm done with it all. I don't want to play anymore."

"Easy, Sid. It's all just part of the game. Now it's your turn to..."

"No. I'm done. Finished. I've been their ping-pong ball for much too long. You know, I really loved all of it once. And I think I could have been good, really good; but with Carla it was always about positioning and marketing and with mother it was always about being the best and nothing less. They drained the joy right out of it. I don't know what I'm doing anymore or why."

Thorne looks a little surprised. Not terribly interested, but surprised, nonetheless. "I wasn't anticipating that response but – whatever. I guess mother will probably be upset. You know she lives through you."

"No. She lived through Carla."

"Wrong again. You're the one. The favorite. Carla was her rival. As for me," he says as he smoothes the cuff of his shirt, "I'm nothing. An extra in the movie of the Chase-Montgomery family.

As she studies her brother at that moment, Sidney wonders if she's ever seen anyone so completely without purpose. So invisible.

"Thorne. You can quit too."

He looks at her and, for a moment, there's possibility in the air, but just as quickly, it disappears.

"And do what? Get an actual job? Work for a living? No, Sid. Very touching. Very Oprah and all that; but the reality is, this is who I am. I don't know how to do anything and I don't care to learn."

He stubs out his cigarette as he gets up from the couch. "I'll report back to mother that her living daughter is no longer an art forger. I won't tell her about you quitting art completely. Not just yet. I think I'll save that one."

Thorne heads for the door. "You know, you're very interesting, Sid. Full of surprises. If I didn't know better, I'd swear you were the half sister –"

She glares at him.

"– on the other hand, utilizing the drama of the moment is very much like mother, herself, isn't it? Yes...very interesting, indeed."

When Thorne reaches the front door, he turns back towards his sister, "Just so you know, we're fully aware of the rest of the forgery ring. Lambykins and Leo. I've already seen them and I think everyone's clear that business is over. Always a pleasure, Sis. I'll see you at Christmas or Easter, whichever comes first."

And with that, he's gone.

43. Reading Between the Lines

And...breathe.

"Poor Ms. Vespry," says I.

"Poor Leo," says Kate.

"Poor Carla."

We're having coffee in Kate's apartment amid all the piles of her many books. It's the morning after our bizarre night on the town, which included a second murder.

"Never have I seen so many poor rich people." Kate stirs more skim milk into her coffee, as she tries to maintain her casual air.

"Leo wasn't rich."

"He was on his way."

"True. But he still wasn't one of them."

"No, you're right." She holds her mug with both hands, letting the warmth comfort her. "I don't know if Ms. Vesprey will ever be the same."

"She'll be fine. She *is* one of them. All of this is just a momentary setback."

So much had happened in such a short time. There's so much to absorb – the Conrads, Hugo's gallery, *Endive*, Shawn Patrik and Victor Conrad, Carla's apartment, the fake paintings, and finally, Leo Ventura's loft, where we discovered a very shaken Eleanor Vespry and a very dead Leo Ventura.

Eleanor Vesprey had phoned the police, and while we waited for them to arrive, she told us the story of *Montgomery Masterpieces*.

"It started innocently, almost as a whim," she said, hands fluttering, "then it grew and grew, becoming quite a lucrative little sideline. At the beginning, Carla handled the procurement of the paintings and I had no idea who created them. When Carla revealed that it was her sister, Sidney, who was the chameleon, I was stunned, as you can imagine. I thought, like everyone else who knew them, that the Montgomery girls loathed each other. Apparently, that was not the case."

She smoothed her hair as she subconsciously clicked the fingernails of her left hand.

"Carla handled all of the dealings with Sidney – Sidney and I didn't, shall we say, care for one another. As the enterprise grew, there became entirely too much for Sidney to produce. That's when Carla brought Leo into the fold." She cleared her throat, "Leo was Carla's newest...hobby. In addition to his obvious charms, she had found that he was technically facile, and saw this as an opportunity from which all could benefit. Leo joined Sidney in creating our product. Their paths rarely crossed, as far as I know, but each was aware of the other's participation.

"Everything we did was totally legal, you must understand, but discretion was still the key for everyone involved. If revealed inappropriately, the implications could be shattering to our careers. I can hear them now – 'If Lamb Vesprey deals in fake art does she deal in fake antiques as well?'...'What is the value of Carla Montgomery's opinions on culture when she blatantly mocks and manipulates it to suit her needs?'...'Sidney who?'...'Leo the hack?' – *not to mention what it could do to the reputations of our clients. Devastating!*

"After a while, Carla and I agreed it had gone on long enough. It was no longer fun, and the risk was growing. There were just a few remaining commissions to be created and/or delivered and then we would be done with it all. Our own private joke. A harmless amusement.

"Then Carla was killed," she traced the picture frame charm dangling from her bracelet. "The police were investigating, others were...too curious. I thought I should put an end to everything immediately before the investigation got any closer and our little sideline was misunderstood. Last night I paid a visit to Sidney's loft, curious, I must admit, about the reception I would be given. But Sidney didn't answer. She must have been out for the evening. I waited a little while before departing and moving on to Leo's loft.

"When I arrived at Leo's, I found the front door slightly open. I called his name, but there was no answer, so I let myself in. Lights were on, music was playing – some dreadful rap or whatever it's called – everything seemed normal until...I discovered Leo's body in the bedroom. It was..." she looked away, touching the fingers of her left hand to her lips, shaking her head slowly, side to side.

"And that is all I know. I phoned the police and then the two of you appeared."

Once the police arrived, we watched as she repeated her story, then we were asked a series of questions. One of the policemen received a phone call from Detective Maroney, after which he turned to us and said, "You can go now. Detective Maroney said to tell you he'd be in touch tomorrow morning."

So here we sit – preoccupied, tired, drinking coffee, taking it all in...and waiting to hear from Detective Jerry.

"You certainly nailed the forgery idea," says Kate, "Very impressive."

"Call it a hunch. I still can't believe Sidney was a part of it, though. She's always been very serious about her work, as far as I know."

"The things we do for money, and, apparently, a lot of money at that."

"True...Carla Montgomery and Eleanor Vesprey selling fakes. What's the world coming to?"

"An end. Just like my coffee. More?"

"Yes, thanks. So...first Carla. Now Leo. Obviously connected?"

"Same weapon."

"Right. And perhaps the same motive. Who would want them both dead? What about Ms. Vesprey herself?"

"Well," Kate returns, coffees in hand, "she's mean enough and bitter enough and delusional enough, but I don't think she's physically strong enough. That woman needs to eat a meal one of these days." In spite of the attitude, Kate looked a little wobbly.

"Kate?"

"I've never seen a dead body before, much less a murdered one."

"Are you all right?"

"No. But I will be." She sipped her coffee. "We have to figure this out, Able. There's a sick-o out there and he – or she – has to be stopped. Let's look at all the possibilities. I'll go first."

"Of course you will."

"Of course I will. We agree that Lambykins is a No?"

I nod.

Kate goes on, "What about the Conrads? Either one? They both had reasons to kill Carla, but Leo?"

"Victor could have been jealous of Leo. Carla dumped him for the newer model..."

"After what we saw last night, I think Victor is very comfortable in Shawn's warm embrace and couldn't care less about the newer model. And as for Becka – well, it's all just too messy for her. Picture her apartment and wardrobe and posture and carefully shaped eyebrows. She's just too neurotically perfect for all this gore, don't you think?"

"I agree on all counts. So that's two more in the NO column. Who else? What about Nan Gibson?"

"Be careful how you talk about my new best friend. The more we learn, the more I find it difficult to believe she even knows these people."

"Social status has its responsibilities."

"Way too much work and not enough fun by a long shot. I think I become happier every day, knowing I'm not that kind of important. You, on the other hand, walk a pretty fine line, Mr. Capital A Artist."

"That's me all right. A legend in your midst. You know, I can get a window table at Chipotlé any time I want? And that's just one of the many perks of being me."

"Don't brag."

"No brag. Just fact. But getting back...Nan Gibson. I say a definite No."

"No argument from me. Which leads us to Shawn Patrik. Passion? Jealousy? Maybe he had a thing for Leo. Maybe he had a thing for Carla! How about that?"

"Possible. But I don't buy it. Shawn is very happy being Shawn. He's not at all conflicted, sexually or otherwise. If he wanted Leo he would have had him, and we've already established Leo could be had. And when it comes to Carla, if Shawn was jealous of Carla at all, it was only because of her shoes."

Kate looked my way and pursed her lips, "Meow," she said.

"Bitchy?"

"Just a little around the edges. We've gotta get you back to the country and all that fresh air." She sips her coffee. "So far we have a lot of 'No's. Who are we leaving out?"

I'm standing by the window, when I look down on the ledge and see an old photograph of Kate as a child sitting with her brother and one of her sisters on a beach.

"Her family."

44. Family Ties

Everybody smile.

Kate looks uncomfortable at the thought. "Do you really think? I mean...oh, that's too awful."

"Agreed. But they're not exactly *Leave It to Beaver*, you said so yourself."

"I'm getting a flashback of our little visit with the Montgomerys: the callous younger brother, the off-putting sister, the alcohol-fueled, cold-blooded mother. Okay, they're a dysfunctional mess, but I can't see a reason for any of them to...to go to all this trouble. I mean they're WASPS from Philadelphia, for heaven's sake. No offense."

"None taken. I may be a WASP, but it's strictly a lower case w. If you're referring to their old money reserve, I know what you mean..."

The phone rings and it's Detective Jerry. Kate picks up up. "Good morning, DJ...yes, we're both here. Able stayed in town last night...that would be fine...we'll see you in a few minutes." Kate puts down the phone. "He's a few blocks away and coming over. How do I look?"

"Fresh as the morning dew."

"Damp? I look damp?"

"Relax, Kate. I don't think it's that kind of a visit."

Kate shakes out her hair, sets her coffee cup down on the end table and starts fluffing pillows. "After 35, every visit is *that kind of a visit*."

Detective Jerry arrives carrying three large grey envelopes. He hands one to each of us and keeps the third for himself.

"Very *Mission Impossible*," says Kate. "What have we here?"

"We'll get to that in a minute. First, how are you both after last night?" he looks genuinely concerned. "It's a lot to deal with."

"I think we're okay, right Kate?"

"Yes," she says, "I think so."

"You handled Ms. Vesprey and the entire situation like a couple of pros. The police were impressed. I wasn't surprised," the detective looks proud of his apprentices.

"Now, Able, if I may...talk to me about art."

"Oh. Well, to begin with, the apartment, Carla's apartment – we studied everything on the walls..."

Kate interrupts, "*He* studied everything. I had no idea what I was looking at. Coffee DJ?"

"Yes, please."

I continue. "Carla's apartment. Every painting by a household name – Whistler, Kline, O'Keefe, Matisse – is a fake, and a very good one."

"You're certain?"

"No doubt about it."

"And they would have fooled you, if you hadn't been looking for something to be wrong?"

"Absolutely. I'm guessing she used her apartment as a showroom, impressing her friends and clients with her fantastic collection, convincing them to let her help them build their own. I'll bet she negotiated the sale of a lot of fakes as the real thing."

"Tell me, if it were to be revealed that these paintings weren't the real thing, what would be the impact do you think?"

"Big. Very big. Carla based her entire career on integrity, honesty, research. My guess is that a lot of people – artists, art collectors, her public – would feel like they'd been duped, that she'd been laughing at them."

Kate returns from the kitchen and hands the detective his coffee. "I've been listening from the other room, and, strictly from a marketing viewpoint, it would be very difficult to put a positive spin on this. Eleanor, Sidney and Leo would have a rough time explaining away their duplicity. Well, maybe not Leo; he could've always taken the poor-young-starving-artist-I-had-to-eat-didn't-I angle. But the other two – definitely damaged goods.

"Carla, on the other hand, would have been fine, because she could have reinvented herself again as an entirely different person – sort of the Anti-Carla. Everything we've been hearing tells me she was done with this part of her life. She was bored with the job, bored with the people and bored with the men. She'd done it all, won in every category and in the end, found it not too difficult and not terribly rewarding."

The detective sips his coffee. "So if this had been revealed, it's your opinion that it could have destroyed Carla's reputation, and she would have been fine with that?"

"Yes, I think so."

"Perhaps even welcomed it?"

"Perhaps."

"Possibly even planned it?" The detective pointed at the grey envelopes laying on the table. We look at them, then at each other, then tear them open.

The detective continues, "These are copies of Carla Montgomery's soon-to-be-published autobiography, in which she thoroughly describes her fake masterpiece operation – starting on page 163 – how it came about, who was involved, how much she enjoyed putting it over on her clientele. She names names and supplies some fairly cruel descriptions of these people."

"Where did you get this?" I ask.

"Last night, I received a message from Karen Richards."

"The agent?" asks Kate. "Was she Carla's?"

"Yes," he looks at Kate. "So you know Karen Richards?"

"Know of her, sure. Powerful. Tough. She and Carla were pretty evenly matched, I'd say."

"Ms. Richards sent over a copy of the manuscript, I read it and met with her this morning. She's tough, as you say, Kate; no nonsense. She didn't care for Carla on a personal level and made that very clear. In fact, she wasn't surprised that someone would have wanted her dead, especially after she saw this manuscript. Having read it, I think I agree with her."

We sit there, flipping through pages, not uttering a sound.

The detective continues, "It's her whole story laid bare. Successes. Failures. Love affairs."

"Is Able mentioned?" asks a suddenly impish Kate.

"Turn to page 146," says the detective. "Able, you're one of the only people that come off well."

"*...went to the Whitney Biennial with Able Ryder, the minimalist artist...*That's it? That's all she says?" asks Kate.

"That's it and that's all. As I said, Able is one of the lucky ones. Basically, the book is an exposé of her unique world and everyone in it. It's informative, as well as cruel; oddly entertaining, as well as purposefully damaging. Scores are obviously being settled here. That's clear. And she didn't care at what personal cost. Half-way through, I found myself thinking, why would someone write something like this? Then, finally, in the last chapter it became clear. I've highlighted the first few paragraphs of it for you to read. If you would, turn to page 245.

45. Picture Perfect: An Unveiling of My Art-Filled Life

by Carla Montgomery

By now you know me or think you do. By now you despise me or think you should. "She has everything," you say to yourself. "She's a spoiled, selfish, self-absorbed bitch, who should be grateful for her good fortune. If I were her," you say, "if I had her opportunities, my life would be perfect."

Perfect. Is that what you think? I'm sure that's the way it looks. I've worked hard to make everything appear perfect. And appearances are, after all, everything. That's what we've all been taught.

We, each and every one of us, present ourselves as carefully composed representations of what we want others to see. I have yet to meet a beautiful person, male or female, who didn't hold their head high and moisten their lips before speaking. I have yet to meet an intelligent person who didn't reference an impressive piece of reading material within the first few minutes of conversation. It's all acting. It's all choreography. Performance art on the well-lit stage we call Public Life.

But there is always more than what the light reveals. The truth, in fact. And the truth lies in the shadows. The dark, seductive, dangerous shadows. In the art world there is a term – chiaroscuro*. It means painting with light and shadow. The artist is able to create depth and mystery by showing us the unseeable, and daring us to crawl inside. Sometimes comforting, sometimes threatening. Always unknown.*

Chiaroscuro. The light and the dark. The clear. The obscure. My world. Welcome to it.

My real name is Ingrid Donner. I was born in a clinic in Zurich, Switzerland. My mother, Katja Donner, was a young girl who worked as a waitress in a restaurant that catered to the many international businessmen who traveled and continue to travel through Switzerland. My father was one of those businessmen, though I've never been able to find out which one. He seduced my mother and left her pregnant. Her family disowned her, her friends abandoned her, her employers dismissed her. She was helpless, ashamed, and alone.

She attempted suicide by jumping from a bridge, but was rescued and taken to a clinic where she was treated and admitted, staying until after her baby was born. The nurses at the clinic took pity on her, more or less adopting her as their own. They took great care of her and, when the time came, of me, her child.

Katja, my mother, was given a job at the clinic as a general assistant. We were given a place to live with two of the nurses. Our lives took on a kind of normalcy, or so I've been told since, until one day, a well-to-do couple from America came. They were young, newly married, and in search of their niece who had been born out of wedlock the previous year and sent to live among us until her mother would be able to return for her. But the mother had died in tragic circumstances, and her sister and brother-in-law had come in her stead.

They had no way of knowing that sadly, the baby, their baby, had also died months before in a flu epidemic. And no one ever told them. Nurses are a clever group; exposed as they are to life's injustices on a daily basis, they seize opportunity when it arises. This was an opportunity for someone – as it turned out, for me.

The nurses explained to my mother that this couple, this privileged American couple, was in search of a child to raise as their own. A child who would want for nothing.

She was young, my mother; young and confused and still racked with guilt. She bought into the lie, renouncing her only child, stoically watching, as she disappeared forever with the attractive, confident, privileged American couple. As her heart ceased to exist, she reminded herself that this was for the best. She was giving her child, her beloved Ingrid, a chance, a true chance, at everything life had to offer.

I left with the Americans that night, too young to understand opportunity or comprehend injustice. Ingrid Donner went into hiding. Carla Montgomery was born.

For five years I was the only child to Cassandra and Charles Montgomery, and life was truly perfect. They doted on me and I adored them. I was much too young to care about the facts or fully understand my recurring memories of a young woman with a soft voice and beautiful, sky blue eyes.

When I was 6, life changed again. My parents, Cassandra and Charles, learned they were expecting a child of their own. They felt this was the right time to explain my genealogy to me. Again, let me repeat, I was 6 years old.

I was told that Daddy Charles was my real father and that my real mother was Penelope, Mother Cassandra's beloved sister. The story went that Penelope had died soon after I was born from complications in delivery, and that her parents had arranged to have me sent to a clinic far away, where I was to be properly cared for until a suitable adoption could be arranged. Charles had never known that I had been born, much less that Penelope had been pregnant.

As fate would have it, he and Cassandra met on their own and fell in love. They married and somehow discovered the truth about Penelope and the baby – even at six, I saw holes in their summation. They vowed that they would find the baby and raise her as their own. And they did…or so they thought. Only time would reveal that there were many half truths being told involving all aspects of my life and its origins.

The only truth that I learned that day and have carried with me ever since is this: I am not who I seem to be.

"Ingrid Donner. Well, how do you like that?" I say to no one in particular.

"I'm speechless," says Kate.

"It'll pass,"I reply.

The detective was watching us closely. "So you really had no idea?"

"None," I say.

"Completely surprised," says Kate.

The detective stands and walks over to the windows. "That's just the beginning of the end of her story. She goes on to explain the inner workings of the Chase Montgomery clan. Here's the abbreviated version: Sidney is born, Cassandra loves her because she's her own flesh and blood, Charles favors Carla because she's the daughter of his true love, Cassandra begins to drink heavily, Charles continues to have affairs, the girls are pitted against each other – Mother's Princess vs. Daddy's Little Girl – which oddly enough makes them closer because they know what their parents are doing, Cassandra has an affair with the groundskeeper to get back at Charles, and that brings us to Thorne."

"You mean..?" I ask, eyebrows halfway up my forehead.

"Yes."

Kate begins to giggle. "So Thorne really is a little bastard."

"In a manner of speaking," says Detective Jerry.

"And all *that* is in the book?"I ask.

"Much more. Sidney's suicide attempts, Cassandra's pill-popping, Thorne's perversities, all for the world to see. I'm guessing if the family found out about this, they wouldn't have been too happy. What do you think?"

We look at each other.

"I don't think Sidney would care," I say. "In fact, I think she'd half expect something like this from Carla."

"As for Thorne, the little bastard,"says Kate, "I think he'd get off on it. It's a chance for him to be a notorious celebrity for a few minutes. It's in keeping with who we already think he is." She sips her coffee, "The grounds keeper's son. You gotta love that. He could sell himself to *Bravo* tomorrow."

"And the parents?" asks the detective.

I think back to the last time I'd seen Charles Montgomery. It was a fundraising event for the Philadelphia Museum, and the Chase Montgomerys were in attendance, Cassandra avidly admiring the Calder mobile, Charles drunkenly admiring the waitresses.

"Charles couldn't care less about anything. He's an empty shell of...an empty shell. He'd probably think it was appropriate that Cassandra was getting her comeuppance. As for Cassandra herself, she would be furious. More than furious. She's old school – never do the family laundry in public."

"Do you think she'd be angry enough to..."

"Kill her daughter? Not possible,"I say, "She's not strong enough or careless enough."

"Getting knocked up by the groundskeeper sounds pretty careless to me," says Kate.

"That was passion, revenge and, no doubt, a little alcohol talking."

"Ditto, ditto, and I repeat, ditto. I agree she isn't strong enough, and I'll add dumb enough to that description; but...what if it was her idea? What if she arranged it? And don't forget, Carla wasn't her daughter. She was the outcome of a family embarrassment involving the man she'd come to hate and the sister, who's memory she had probably come to despise."

We all roll this idea around in our minds, finding unpleasant logic behind it.

"I think it's time to pay another call on the Chase Montgomery family," says the detective.

"It's beginning to sound like another kind of family," I say.

"If you ask me, the only difference between a Mob family and a WASP family is the volume."

As usual, Kate has the last word.

46. Taking the Edge Off

Cold, crisp and neat.

"What's your preference, sir?"

'Knives,' he thinks,'Sharp knives,' but that isn't what she's asking.

"Glenfiddich on the rocks."

"Coming up." The bartender takes the bottle from the shelf behind her and proceeds to pour. She's blonde, pretty, toned within an inch of her life. "You want to run a tab?"

"Sounds good."

She smiles the insincere smile of a practiced service professional. "That eye's gotta hurt," she says cautiously.

He sees his reflection in the bar mirror. His left eye, where Leo had landed a solid blow is becoming more purple and green by the second. He kind of likes seeing himself like this. Rough. Dangerous.

"A gentlemen's disagreement?" she asks.

"I guess you could call it that."

"Did you win?"

He takes a swallow of his scotch, "I killed the guy."

"Good for you," she replies, not realizing he's telling the truth. She smiles again. He likes her smile. It's a tough smile that still manages to look sweet. It reminds him of Carla's smile.

As she goes about straightening the bar, he studies his reflection – the black eye, the torn shirt, the cigarette and scotch before noon. Mother would not approve, he thinks. She would not approve at all. "Appearances, Thorne," she would say. "Never forget who you are. Never forget you're a Chase Montgomery."

He lights another cigarette, not noticing that one is still burning in the ashtray. His foot has begun to tap nervously in that way it always does when he thinks about his mother...

Suddenly he is ten years old again, practicing the piano in the music room. From the doorway he hears the sound of ice cubes in a glass, signalling his mother's arrival.

"So beautiful, Thorne. So very beautiful," she said as she came up behind him. She put down her glass and began stroking his hair. "You're nothing like your father, Thorne. You're a Chase, like I am. We see things, feel things, other people don't."

She ran her right hand slowly down his arm reaching for the fingers still extended on the keys. "Such wonderful fingers, long, delicate; an artist's hands. You'll do great things my angel, my prince." She lowered her head next to his and whispered softly in his ear, "I love you Thorne. I love you most of all. You're the child of my heart." She turned his head to face her, tilted his chin upward, then kissed him slowly, sensually.

It had not been the first time.

He became her pet, her plaything, her confidant, her tool. She manipulated his sense of purpose while mutilating his sense of self. He became alternately desirous and fearful of her affections. There were never any friends while growing up, just mother, Carla, Sidney and the staff. Father made an occasional appearance; but to him, Thorne was invisible.

He became jealous of his mother's relationships with the girls. She connected with them in a different way. They talked, laughed, argued. He thought she loved them more. But late at night, when the rest of the house was asleep, she would come to his room and comfort him, explaining that they needed her guidance and encouragement because they were not fully formed. Sidney, she felt, was more a Montgomery than a Chase and therefore, weak. Fortunately, she'd inherited Cassandra's artistic talents. She would develop Sidney's talents, her gifts, as best she could.

Mother's relationship with Carla was, well, complicated. She never fully trusted her. Ever. Both Sidney and Thorne knew at a very early age that Carla was their half sister, not their mother's daughter by birth. To him, they always seemed to be rivals more than step-mother and step-daughter.

Carla was magic, he thought. Carla was special. She could stand up to mother and did. She was smart and interesting and exuded a kind of force. She tried to be a big sister as much as mother would allow, but as they got older, Carla was distanced from the family. He and Sidney always guessed it was mother's doing, but mother said it was Carla.

When he was 16, he called Carla on it. He went to New York to see her, not telling mother what he was up to. He showed up at her apartment, and she greeted him as she always did. "Hello you," she would say, then kiss his cheek and muss his hair. She was happy to see him. He knew it.

They had a good long talk that day. She made him feel like a friend, like an equal, not just a pain-in-the-ass younger brother. She told him at some point he had to get out on his own, and she would always be there to help in any way she could. But she wouldn't be in Bryn Mawr very much anymore. She was careful not to say anything against mother.

Thorne's foot was tapping faster now.

Carla did like him. He was sure of it. He did go visit her often over the next few years.

Tap. Tap.

Mother always said Carla was laughing at him and thought he was ridiculous.

Tap. Tap.

Carla was so beautiful and so much fun. She had that smile. That tough, sweet smile.

Tap. Tap.

Mother said Carla was cheap, like her mother had been, and that you couldn't trust anything she said.

Tap. Tap. Tap.

Carla wanted him to leave Bryn Mawr, leave mother, come to New York and go to school. She would help. Anything he needed...

Tap. Tap. Tap. Tap. Tap. Tap.

Mother laughed when he told her. "Look how she's treated Sidney," she said. "Look how she's turned her back on the family. She doesn't want to help you, Thorne, she's mocking you. She only thinks of herself. Even now, she's writing a book about all of us, don't ask me how I know. She wants to destroy the entire family and ruin our name. What kind of a person would do such a thing?" Mother had looked distraught when she said this. "If you love your mother, you'll stop her, Thorne. She's not your sister! She's not like you and I!" And then the tears...and then the sobbing...as she collapsed in his arms, no longer the omnipotent protector of the Chase Montgomery dynasty, but a very convincing version of a delicate, desolate creature. "She must be stopped. Do it for me, Thorne. Do it for your mother."

Tap.

And so he had.

"Sir, are you all right?" it was the bartender's voice. "Would you like me to call someone?"

She had awakened him from the nightmare of his memories. His shirt was soaked through with sweat and tears. He no longer looked dangerous. Just pathetic.

"I'm sorry, I'm afraid I'm not feeling very well. Perhaps I should go home and lie down."

"That sounds like a good idea. Can I call you a cab?" her concern was genuine.

"No, no. I'll be fine, really. I'm sorry about all this. You've been very kind. What's your name?"

She looked hesitant for a second, then, "It's Tania."

"Pretty name. Thank you again, Tania."

It was time to go home. To see mother and tell her about his last few days. He had accomplished what she'd wanted him to...and she <u>*had*</u> *wanted him to. He was sure of that.*

They had been in the conservatory...

"Since your unfortunate incident with our Carla..."

"But mother, you wanted..."

"Don't interrupt, Thorne. You were confused. You had one of your spells. You overreacted. It's all right, my darling. I still love you." Cassandra was trimming roses, arranging them in a vase. "Everyone believes it was that young artist who killed her, and why shouldn't they? It's the kind of thing a person like that would do. It was only a matter of time." She spoke in a quiet, hypnotic voice. "Carla was using him the way she used everybody. Yes, I'm sure he would have hurt her eventually. You only have to look at him to see the danger.

"He may threaten the rest of us. He may go after Sidney. That sort is never to be trusted. He's dangerous, Thorne. A threat to the family. You must put an end to him. You must do it for Carla."

Her voice never rose, never changed inflection. She was requesting a second murder as she casually arranged roses. His head was spinning. This woman was his mother. He loved her, he feared her, he hated her and wanted her dead. He'd kill her with her own scissors.

"Thorne, that's an odd expression. Are you feeling all right? I think you need a change of scene. Why don't you drive to New York tomorrow and visit our dear Sidney. You might want to recommend that I would appreciate it if she ceased this embarrassing forgery business Carla got her involved in. Perhaps you could relay the same message to that awful Ms. Vesprey. And do make certain that they know I'm serious, my love. Will you do that for me?

"Oh, and while you're there, you can also pay a call on our artist friend. I think he should be stopped, don't you?" As she plucked a final thorn from its stem, Cassandra admired her arrangement with pride and satisfaction. "A little New York get away...like the secret visits you shared with Carla over the years. Yes, I know all about them. I always have."

He felt a chill run down his spine. Cassandra finished with her flowers and stepped over to him, taking his face in her hands and pulling it close to hers. "Have a wonderful time my angel. And let me know the minute you return." She kissed him, deeply, then studied his face as if it was one of her roses. "Oh, I love my son," she said, "I do. I do."

Thorne ran a hand through his hair then reached in his pocket, took out two one hundred dollar bills and set them on the bar as a tip for the pretty blonde bartender. Mother would have been proud of the gesture. He had remembered who he was. He was Hawthorne William Chase Montgomery, and Chase Montgomerys pay for kindness.

47. Form Follows Disfunction

Making memories.

Visiting the family. That's what Cassandra called it when she took her then small children on a walking tour of their home. She would point out the ancestral portraits, telling stories of this one or that. She would educate them about the aesthetic and historical lineage of various furnishings and objets d'art. They were impressive as a family, when viewed within the confines of legend and memory. In reality, they suffered horribly by comparison – the cold and distant parents, the worthless scoundrel of a husband, the sister Cassandra had once loved, but now saw as uselessly melodramatic. And then there were the children.

Sidney. Her first born. She'd inherited her mother's artistic talents and, unfortunately, her father's complacency. If it hadn't been for Cassandra's constant coaxing, her career would have never happened.

They'd been close when Sidney was a teen – the museum outings, the private "tutorials" – those were good years. Cassandra had watched with pride and amazement as her daughter's capabilities increased and grew. Sidney could be great. Sidney <u>would</u> be great. Cassandra would see to it. But then, after college, her talent, or interest, plateaued. What was worse, she didn't seem to care – so like her father. Cassandra decided she must do something drastic to force Sidney out of her rut. That was when she cut her off financially. She had done the same with Carla, of course for different reasons, and Carla had risen to the challenge, succeeding brilliantly. Cassandra hoped Sidney would respond in a similar fashion.

After a slow start she did, thanks in no small part to the support and guidance and interference of her older sister. Together they succeeded in not only celebrating Sidney's talents and accelerating her rise through the art world, but also in cheapening those same talents with their "imitations" business.

Cassandra was appalled and disgusted when she found out. So disrespectful. So unnecessary. And ultimately, so vulgar. She blamed Carla for the idea, but blamed Sidney for her complete lack of spine in choosing to go along with it. Didn't she realize this could destroy her reputation and discredit the family? Sidney could have been the first of the Chase Montgomerys to become an artistic presence. What a privilege, what an honor. It would mean so much.

Cassandra hoped she wasn't too late to rectify the situation and undo Carla's harmful influence. This would be her main focus now. Sidney would be the next great woman artist, no matter what the cost.

Thorne – fine, beautiful Thorne. Her child of the heart. Her child of revenge. She didn't remember his father's name. She didn't care. It didn't matter. Thorne was her son, hers alone. She raised him to be her heir, her accomplice in life. Cassandra felt that Thorne had a heightened sensibility. She was blind to any of his faults and fooled herself into thinking him a prodigy in all things cultured. She shielded him from the crassness of the everyday, enveloping him in a world of her own making. Thorne was her pet, her plaything, her project.

He alone understood the awkward position Carla had put them all in. He alone understood the importance of the family identity. He had handled the Carla situation – albeit heavy-handedly – but he'd done it for her, for his mother, the one true woman in his life. He'd done as she wished.

And now he'd taken care of that knife artist as well. What, she wondered was more precious than a son's love?

Cassandra never questioned the excessiveness of her involvement or the inappropriateness of her affections. Thorne was not like other children. Why should he be treated like them? She was a mother nurturing her special child. A gifted mother. A gifted child.

Carla – not her own flesh and blood, not her sister's either, as it turned out. That's what eventually drove them apart. The deceit of it all. Cassandra was convinced Carla had known the truth for a long time and was playing her for a fool. That could not be tolerated, so when the truth was revealed, Carla was removed from the nuclear family.

She was the best of them, though, and Cassandra knew it. She was the most like her. Effortlessly beautiful, bright, intuitive. She had lived the life Cassandra had planned to live, filled with important people and cultural ties. Cassandra was jealous of Carla's existence and knew it. More so, she was hurt and angered by the callous disregard with which Carla viewed everything of true importance. She had no idea how privileged she was, nor how enormous a responsibility privilege carries. But Carla was always Carla, and that meant charming as well as calculating, fascinating as well as cold. She had enjoyed Carla's successes and notoriety in spite of herself, even taking pride in them. For Carla was still the daughter of Cassandra Chase Montgomery to the outside world, and maintaining the family legend was all-important.

If only she hadn't written that book, exposing their private lives for everyone to see. That was a mistake. A very unfortunate mistake. But the mistake had been dealt with and now the wounds would mend.

So this was her family; her ancestors and progeny. Each, more useless than the next. She'd wasted her life. It was obvious now. To the world at large she was all things bright and beautiful. In her own heart of hearts, Cassandra Chase Montgomery was a complete and utter void.

There had been a time – before the children, before the marriage, before Penelope's suicide – there had been a time when her options for happiness seemed limitless. She would marry – or not. Become an artist – or not. Travel – or not. Nothing definite, no responsibilities, but life turned out differently. She could blame the children for tying her down, blame Charles for stealing her youth, blame her parents for never expressing love or pride or anything resembling a human emotion.

"And now I've become my mother <u>and</u> my father."

She laughed at the overwhelming irony. She had become everything she despised – a tough business mind like her father who placed more importance on the power of the family than on the family itself; an imposing social presence like her mother, who polished and perfected outer appearances, while letting the inner workings decay beyond repair; a parent like both of them, who was hated, feared and, ultimately, unknown to her own children. Theirs was a family of strangers. It always had been. It would continue to be.

Cassandra looked at her watch, a platinum and diamond Patek Phillipe. It had belonged to her mother and her grandmother before that. It always kept perfect time. It wouldn't dare not to.

The detective would arrive shortly with Able Ryder and the young lady. What did they know or think they knew? What did they understand about the responsibilities of a privileged life? Oh, it was all so tiresome. The family was once again on display to be studied, dissected and judged. Cassandra had a job to do, her most important job, as she saw it – keeper of the Chase Montgomery flame. She must appear sensitive, serene, caring, motherly. She studied her reflection in the rococo Venetian mirror to her right.

"I'd better change," she said.

48. Every Rose...

A delicate flower.

Thorne was in his bathroom trying without success to hide his many bruises and abrasions, psychic as well as physical. He heard his mother walk past his rooms, down the hallway to her suite. It would be just the two of them today entertaining their unwanted visitors. Mother and son. Partners in life. He'd done everything for her, just as she'd known he would. She'd thanked him for defending the family honor. She'd shown her appreciation.

Thorne mashed out another cigarette in the soap dish he used as an ashtray. His head was spinning. Remembering. Reliving. Trying to make sense of the senseless past.

He'd gone to see Carla that night. He'd spoken to her about the book, just as mother had asked. Carla said that it was too late to change anything, not that she would have, even if it were possible. She explained that there were a few family secrets revealed but nothing earth-shattering. "You worry too much, little brother," she'd said, "everything will be fine, just fine. You'll see. A little fresh air, that's all."

They'd hugged and kissed goodbye. She'd been in a hurry, getting ready for a night out. He'd never seen her more beautiful.

As he got into the elevator, he looked back to see her standing in her doorway. She blew him a kiss on her index finger, then smiled that smile. The elevator doors closed.

Fifteen minutes later Thorne was headed for home and Carla was lying dead in a growing pool of blood.

It was mother who told him she'd been found dead and she thought he'd done it. She was fine with that. More than fine, she was pleased, so he didn't bother denying it.

And then came Leo. He'd never meant to kill him, just scare him a little, that was all. But Leo laughed at him. He laughed. Thorne lost control. His temper flared. He wanted to stop Leo, to shut him up. He saw the knife on the table, grabbed it and started stabbing wildly. Over and over. Again and again. He was in a blind rage. When he regained control, when the noises in his head had stopped, when he saw Leo's body covered in blood, he realized what he'd done. Thorne was caught up in a bad dream and there was no waking up.

Mother was going to take him down. He knew it. He could feel it. She was going to let the detective and his sidekicks believe it was all his doing, all his idea – Carla, Leo, the cover up...

His twitch had returned – a subtle blinking of his left eye. Most people never noticed, but to Thorne it felt like the flapping of an eagle's wing. Mother had something to do with all of this, he was sure of it. But she would glide above it, as she always did, and let him take the blame for everything. And there was nothing he could do about it.

How could anyone understand that he was powerless; that his mother, this petite, attractive, mature blonde in the cashmere twin set and pearls, controlled his every action. Years of rewards coupled with punishment, praise with criticism, clashes with caresses had left him emotionally wrecked and confused. Thorne knew what he was. There was no denying it and there was no changing it either. The outside world wouldn't care about the psychological underpinnings. To them he would be seen as a murderer plain and simple. Not a family protector. Not a dutiful son. Not a stunted victim himself. He had killed and he must pay.

He would go downstairs when the time came and play his part. He would tell his story and let them think what they may. But first there was a visit to be made. A meeting to be had. He would go down the hall and see mother.

Thorne opened his bedroom door. There was someone waiting on the other side.

"Hello you," his visitor said.

"Jesus! You startled me! I didn't know you were here. We're meeting with the detective in a couple of minutes. Did you want to –"

He never saw the knife.

49. The Ties That Bind

The same, but different.

"Mrs. Vesprey called this morning to report a visit she had from Thorne Montgomery," The detective is bringing us up to date as we drive toward Bryn Mawr. "It was when she went home from Leo Ventura's the night he was killed. Thorne was waiting for her, in the shadows outside her building. He said he needed to talk to her. She said it wasn't a good time. He forced the issue. Apparently he demanded that she put an end to the fake masterpiece business, saying she'd be very sorry if she didn't. Ms. Vesprey tried to explain that it was over and done with, but he didn't seem to listen. She said he looked agitated and nervous.

"He said to her, 'My mother and I aren't happy. Do you understand? I've already been to see your artists. I think they understand.' He left her on the sidewalk, hopped a cab and disappeared, leaving Ms. Vesprey shaking on the street. She ran to her apartment, bolted the door and phoned Sidney.

"Sidney answered. Keep in mind these two women have supposedly never liked each other. She told Sidney about Leo and about her run-in with Thorne. Sidney, according to Ms. Vesprey, was shocked and frightened by the news. She, in turn, told Ms. Vesprey about her own visit from Thorne that same evening. They agreed that they had to notify the police."

"Thus, the phone call," says Kate.

"Exactly."

"So we're still thinking along the lines of family ties? Cassandra or Thorne?" I ask.

Kate, who's sitting in the back seat, catches the detective's expression in the rear view mirror.

"Or Sidney," she says. "Of course!"

"Of course?" I repeat. "This morning we were all set on Cassandra, next all things point to Thorne, now it's Sidney? Of course?"

"Wait, wait," she says. "Let me think...Sidney was jealous of Carla's success...too simple; she was jealous of her beauty...no, Sidney knows how attractive she is. Not success. Not beauty. Certainly not money...it had to be a man...Sidney was jealous of...Leo! Is that it? Sidney was hot for Leo! No...no...no...Sidney was in love with Leo!

"Detective, what did Carla write about Leo in her book?"

The detective looked impressed. "She described him as a no-talent hustler; the kind of pretty boy hack all too common in the art world today. She said his only real talent was between his legs, so that's what she used him for."

"Sidney must have found out, but who told her? Carla? No, not Carla. The book agent, what's her name? No, she couldn't have cared less. It was, it was...Cassandra! Cassandra told her, hoping to stir up trouble? No. Hoping to get Sidney to plead with Carla to not publish the book? That's it! But it backfired, or did it? They argued. Or maybe Sidney was already on the edge when she got to the apartment. At any rate, she killed her. She killed her sister."

"But why would Cassandra tell Sidney about Leo? Why would she think she'd care?" I ask.

Kate catches the detective's eye in the mirror again. "Because Sidney was sleeping with Leo. They were having an affair, weren't they detective?"

"We found evidence at Leo's loft that supports that theory, yes."

"So, not only did Sidney love Leo. Leo loved Sidney back," says Kate, very proud of herself.

"But how did Cassandra know?" I ask.

"Oh Able," says a very superior-sounding Kate, "women know everything. That should be obvious to you by now."

50. Too Little, Too Late

A problem shared...

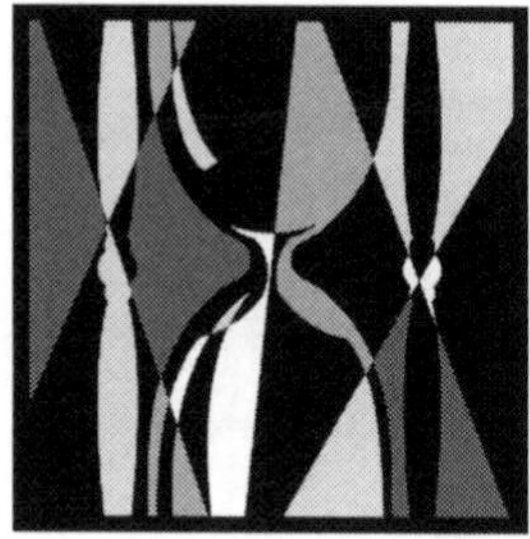

When we arrive at the Chase Montgomery home, we're ushered into the garden room. Cassandra is standing by the windows, looking out over the great lawn. She doesn't seem to notice us.

Detective Jerry begins to speak, "Mrs. Montgomery, thank you for taking the time to..."

"Sidney used to sketch the trees when she was a child," Cassandra interrupts, "for hours on end. Very good drawings, too. I kept them all." She turns and faces her guests. "Good afternoon. Won't you please sit down?"

"Mrs. Montgomery, will your son be joining us?" asks Detective Jerry.

She looks at him – through him actually – then turns to Kate. "Do you want children, Miss Lindsey? They're a blessing you know. But motherhood is very...*difficult*. You want always to protect them from..." she looks to Able. "Your parents must be very proud of you Able. Are they? Are they proud?"

I shoot a quick glance at Kate, then say,"I like to think so. I hope they're as proud of me as I am proud of them."

"Proud of them, you say?" Cassandra smiles an odd, weak half smile then turns away.

The three of us look at each other with an uncomfortable concern. I break the silence.

"Cassandra, is Thorne here? Are you all right? Has something happened?"

"Has something happened?" she repeats, as if speaking to ghosts, "Life happened."

Cassandra suddenly looks very small.

"Cassandra?" I say softly, comfortingly.

"Thorne is upstairs...with his sister."

Detective Jerry runs to the foyer and up the staircase. Kate stands frozen, not quite sure what's happening – imagining the worst, hoping it isn't true. I step over to catch Cassandra, as she stumbles and falls into my arms. Together, we ease her into the nearest chair.

"Are you okay here?" I ask Kate.

"Yes,"she says, as calmly as she can. She puts her arm around Cassandra's shoulder. I take off in search of the detective. When I reach the top of the stairs, I follow the sound of his voice and find him in what must have been Thorne's room standing over his lifeless body.

"...two bodies. Upstairs," the detective says into his phone.

"Two?" I ask. But I already know.

"Sidney. Down the hall in her mother's bedroom."

She'd been shot at close range. The gun is on the table – a small silver pistol, a lady's gun. Sidney lies on the floor at the foot of the bed. She's still holding a blood-stained knife.

Downstairs, Kate is cautiously comforting Cassandra. The house is uncomfortably quiet. Kate is putting the pieces together, not wanting to believe what she thinks has happened.

"Mothers are never supposed to have a favorite," Cassandra speaks in a soft, measured tone. "We do, of course, but it's our responsibility to make certain no one suspects. Sidney was always my favorite. I don't think she ever knew."

" 'Was my favorite,' repeats Kate. "And so it's true."

51. Completing the Picture

A problem shared...

"I always wanted brothers and sisters growing up, but now I'm feeling pretty good about the 'only child' thing."

Kate's sitting at the kitchen counter, nursing her martini and choosing her next hors d'oeuvre. Peggy Lee sings softly in the background – *All or Nothing at All*. Days have passed since our final call on the Chase Montgomerys. Cassandra eventually told her story, making it sound more like a string of unfortunate events rather than the horror show it was.

Cassandra had sent Sidney to see Carla that night long ago. She did ask her to plead with her sister to not publish the book. Sidney didn't care. She told her Carla was laughing at all of them – Sidney didn't care. She told her about the passages that made a mockery of Sidney's talent – again, she didn't care. She told her Carla had portrayed Leo as a fool, a no-talent, a cheap hustler – something snapped. Sidney killed her sister that night – and she didn't care.

After all the extremes of their sisterly relationship – the love, the hate, the jealousies – Carla had attacked the one person Sidney had ever loved; the only person who had ever truly loved her back. It was enough.

Cassandra had also sent Thorne to do her bidding and mistakenly assumed he was responsible for Carla's death. She hadn't thought him capable of such a thing and felt oddly proud. She sent him to see Leo and Lamb Vesprey to handle the forgery business embarrassment. Thorne killed Leo in a pathetic attempt to please his mother.

When Sidney found out about Leo's murder, she bacame completely undone. She left a long, rambling letter which was found in her loft. In the letter, she took responsibility for her sister' death and targeted her brother and mother, explaining that her family needed to be destroyed. She came home one last time to kill her brother and mother, and then herself.

She succeeded with Thorne, but Cassandra changed the final outcome. When she saw Sidney's reflection in her vanity mirror, when she saw the knife in her hand, she calmly reached in her drawer, pulled out her small handgun and defended herself against her favorite child.

"How's your drink?" I ask.

"Smaller than it used to be."

"Let me fix that...I think we should have a toast. Here's to –"

"Motherly love."

"I'll drink to that."

"Of course you will. Your mother's wonderful."

"So's yours."

"Well, I didn't used to think so," says Kate."However, in light of recent events, I've come to believe she's pretty wonderful herself. You know, she never tried to kill me, not even once, and Lord knows I've given her enough reasons. Seriously though, what happens to Cassandra now?"

"DJ says she's had a complete mental collapse and has been taken to a private institution."

"A luxury spa, no doubt."

"No doubt. Not that it really matters. It seems she's completely unaware of her surroundings. Doesn't speak, doesn't eat, just stares off into the distance occasionally muttering something about her beautiful children. She's a woman in ruins."

"Amazing," says Kate, shaking her head and twirling her olive. "Do we know what's happened to the husband?"

"Apparently, when he was told everything, he let out a pathetic laugh, had a massive heart attack and died instantly."

"Incredible. I'm guessing he's not an ideal organ donor. Really awful, though, right? I mean, it's *beyond* Shakespearean...what's beyond Shakespearean.....it's *Homeric*!"

"You never cease to surprise me."

"Stop. I'm on a roll. Cassandra's main purpose in life was to protect the family at all costs and now the family is completely gone. The rich *are* different from you and me."

"You're just finding that out?"

"No, really. They're nuts! Totally insane. I've gotta thank you, Able. I'm always thanking you for something – usually food and tips for removing stains – but getting involved in this experience with you has really opened my eyes up to a lot of things."

"For instance?"

"Well, like I'm smarter than I give myself credit for."

"True."

"And I'm a lot more fortunate than I realize."

"Very true."

"And you're my family, Able. You."

"Absolutely true."

"It's good to be us, don't you think?"

"Yes, it is. And yes, I do," we clink glasses again. "Who needs wealth and power when you've got good friends, good conversation, good music and good vodka. How's that martini?"

"Perfect," Kate eats the last olive and swallows the last delicious drop,"...and done."

Made in the USA
Middletown, DE
07 August 2016